JAIL

JAIL

JESÚS ZÁRATE

TRANSLATED FROM THE SPANISH BY
GREGORY RABASSA

ALIFORM PUBLISHING
MINNEAPOLIS

ALIFORM PUBLISHING
is part of the Aliform Group
117 Warwick Street SE/Minneapolis, MN USA 55414
information@aliformgroup.com   www.aliformgroup.com

Originally published in Spanish as *La cárcel*
Editorial Planeta: Barcelona, 1972
Premio Planeta, 1972

First published in the United States of America by
Aliform Publishing, 2003

Library of Congress Control Number
2003093940

ISBN 0-9707652-3-1

Printed in the United States of America
Set in Times New Roman
Cover art by Lourdes Cué
Cover design by C.Fox Design

CONTENTS

JAIL

I
THE RAT

WEDNESDAY, OCTOBER 14

This is the definition of the law: something that can be broken.
  Gilbert K. Chesterton

My name is Antón Castán.

My name is really Antonio Castán, but when I was quite young in school my classmates, by cordial consent, decided to despoil the word of its last two letters, useless letters, and ever since I myself have tossed them away into the realm of oblivion.

Far from deforming my personality, that verbal mutilation has defined and fulfilled it. Antón characterizes me in a civil way since it holds on to the essence of my true name and at the same time it idealizes the ordinariness of Antonio a bit.

Antonio is a name for a patrician or a saint and I have nothing of one or the other. Antón is closer to my authentic inclinations as it is a name for a revolutionary or a prisoner. While it is the accepted and everyday form of my legal identification, at the same time it is my *nom de guerre*. Being named Antón is like carrying a banner through life.

Antonio is a name to be inscribed in the national census. It's a name for tax statistics and real estate assessments. Antón on the other hand, is a name for letters, the old-fashioned way of describing something that implies intellectual activity. Antón would be a fine pseudonym for someone writing poetry or novels.

Mister Alba told me one day:

"Antonio is a name that has decadent Latin cadences. Antón is a name with a mystical Slavic precision. You did well to change your name. In this jail, the same as in the history of Rome, all heroes are named Antonio."

As I'm not a Latinist but have been perforce by accidental assimilation, Antón serves as the release from a bond. The word, sharp as a military command, is my name and my nickname at the same time. This duality breaks my ties to the spiritual limitations of a race and a people and makes me what I really want to be: an insignificant yet substantial part of humanity.

I've mentioned a bond, chains. There'll be a lot of talk of chains in this book. Maybe that's the secret of my complacent acceptance of being so baptized. Antonio was the name imposed on me by the law of long family tradition, cultural and religious, unavoidable and established. Antón is the name with which I break that law. Antón was the name given me by friendship, meaning freedom.

Antón is the only way I have left to be free.

When I was what they call a free man none of this concerned me very much. Under a regime of individual choice it doesn't matter what you call yourself. Under those conditions you're even allowed that beautiful bastard luxury of having no name or surname. It's enough just to know that you're a human being.

In jail, when I touch my body and search out my soul, all I find is the protuberance that's the remnant of my name and that's a consolation now. Jail has despoiled me of everything except a conviction that still survives in the bosom of my consciousness. The conviction that I can still feel like a free man despite the number they've marked me with here. I still have a life preserver left because I've got the intimate refuge of my name that preserves the certainty that I still belong to the human race.

THURSDAY, OCTOBER 15

Where would we end up if we started right off
talking about our innocence?
    Franz Kafka

I don't know why I decided to begin this book. Pure and
simple, with no concrete aim, like someone just turning on
a water faucet, yesterday I got to writing it.

Yesterday I completed three years in jail. Maybe the
gloomy milepost of this anniversary can explain the unconscious impulse that brought me to undertake this task.

It's become impossible now for me to give it up. The
river of my voice won't stop flowing.

I have at my disposal a pencil and a few sheets of paper
that David gave me. The biggest problem is keeping the
point of the pencil sharp. For that I had to call upon a jailer,
who doesn't seem all that kindly disposed to collaborate.
I'll have to gauge my inspiration in accord with the extent
of the jailer's kindness or whim. In jail talent is a little
dependent on the tip of a pencil.

The urge to write something had been working on me
for several weeks, even though I hadn't decided on what
means I should adopt to transmit my thoughts and put my
experiences and memories in order. Poetry calls for the

gift of cosmic prophecy, which I lack. A novel is a mirror along the road, as Stendhal said, and in jail there's neither mirror nor road. Theater would be more adequate; theater mimics life so badly that it always frightens me more than life itself. Memoirs are a form of vengeance on the part of statesmen in decline or a coquetry of public relations for proper ladies. The essay is journalistic philosophy, which is like saying irreligious religion.

I was left with no recourse but a diary. And I'm not sorry. In spite of also being discredited, a diary is the instrument of the most honest expression because it's the only one which knows right from the beginning that it's not sincere. It doesn't pretend to prophesy like poetry, or collaborate with madness like the novel, or aspire to supplant the truth like theater, or put on makeup like memoirs, or assume the pose of a pedant like the essay. It shares in the ingredients of all those styles, however, the good and the bad, but in careful doses. Among them all, a diary is the most inoffensive way to lie.

Besides, since jail is as true and as false as literature itself, a diary is the literary genre *par excellence* for prisoners. It doesn't demand so much that we say something. It doesn't require us to think, but only to fill the solitude and silence with words. It doesn't make us run on like journalism (thinking about running in jail has got to be ironic). A diary can be the camera of popular cinematography, the everyday note of a shopkeeper, the instant picture of a street photographer, the lyrical puberty of a girl, the incisive bookkeeping of someone starving to death. It's probably because it's so easy that even men who haven't been in jail have written diaries.

I've worn down the point of my pencil. The jailer's off somewhere and since it's late I can't shout for him.

Mister Alba has taken off his shirt. He's getting ready for sleep. Without his shirt on, I don't know why, his lack of an eye becomes more noticeable on his face. His belly shows a bright tattoo that perfectly reproduces the blade of a straight razor. Two or three rolls of wavy fat hide or reveal it according to Mister Alba's respiratory will.

It's a very expressive tattoo on a prisoner who's not a murderer. That stomach tattoo has always caught my attention because the chest and arms are ordinarily the preferred field for that kind of epidermal paleography. As he sees me hesitating with my pencil hovering over the paper, Mister Alba raises his hand to his tattoo. Something that I just can't believe happens then right before my eyes. Like someone taking off his glasses, Mister Alba removes the tattoo and places in my hand the blade of a razor with no handle or sheath but with a plastic cover over the cutting edge. It's a genuine blade. What looked like a tattoo before is quite real.

I look at the razor and then at Mister Alba's eyes. I realize that what Mister Alba has revealed to me is not a Chinese sketch on his skin but is in fact a blade-shaped incision, a pouch in his flesh where the weapon is kept as it then takes on completely the look of a tattoo. It's a perfect job of a metal inlay in a human body. A dentist couldn't have made a work of art like that in a molar.

"I had it done in Panama," Mister Alba explains. "I'll tell you later how they went about it."

And he smiles proudly as I begin to sharpen the point of the pencil.

I speak to him in a low voice.

"It's funny they haven't discovered it."

"And they'll never discover it just so long as they don't touch me," Mister Alba replies. "A cop frisks a prisoner all over. Everywhere except the stomach. The law only touches the stomachs of women."

FRIDAY, OCTOBER 16

Being free is not wanting to do what one wants,
but wanting to do what one can.

 Jean-Paul Sartre

Lying on the cot when I've just opened my eyes I perceive
the assiduous and familiar bustle.

I look at the brick floor, which has ended up losing its
original russet sheen since it hasn't been scrubbed. There's
the shoe.

Before I found out what the secret spring or unknown
energy was that made it move, watching the shoe day after
day took up a whole period of passing time that might be
considered the happiest, if such a word is fitting here, of
my three years of confinement. The stupid lethargy of
imprisonment was broken for a spell by the bright perspective of the miracle. The shoe that walked by itself
represented for me the gateway to poetry, the promise of
freedom, the gratification of illusion, the escape; in short,
to everything that jail had taken away from me. Since there
was a mystery I went back to being a man, and not just any
man but a creature drawn to the inexplicable by the miraculous thread of fantasy.

All of it is repeated each morning. I wake up, and as
though my act of leaving sleep were communicated to the

shoe by means of some invisible antenna, the shoe automatically begins to move. A short time later the rat sticks out its damp snout filled with funny little baby teeth. It looks at me with a kind of irrationally human mockery and with a leap it dives into the tunnel that leads to its banquet of garbage. In some way the rat has discovered that this is a jail, a forbidden zone, and that it has the honor of being the companion of Mister Alba. Therefore, it behaves like an exceptional rat, sleeping in the jail by night and marauding through freedom's garbage by day.

Of the four of us who share the cell, Braulio Coral has an open antipathy toward the rat. Braulio is jealous of the rat. David Fresno, on the other hand, likes it, the same as I. As for Mister Alba, that's a different story. Mister Alba has tried to domesticate it.

One afternoon after he had been out of the cell, when Mister Alba got back he took a metal chain from his pocket, a chain like the ones used to tie up dogs but much thinner and more delicate.

"What's that?" David asked him.

"In proletarian language it's a symbol of oppressive capitalism, forged from silver, or shall we say a chain of excess profits."

"What?"

"In Marxist parlance, a chain of silver."

"How did you get it past without their finding it?"

"I took advantage of the hour of the dollar."

"What's the hour of the dollar?"

"The time when jailers can't see."

"I can't see what you'd want with a chain."

"What else could it be for? To tie up the rat."

"Are you going to tame it?"

"A prisoner in the United States, a fellow named Stroud, became famous from breeding canaries, which are a symbol of freedom. Of course this Stroud dreamed of getting his freedom back so he could get a cage and keep on being jailer to the canaries. I don't hope to fly as high as Stroud. I know the ground I'm walking on. I'm going to tame rats, which are a symbol of jail. I'll sell them to prisoners. It'll be nice to watch them walking the rats, holding on to the rats' leashes."

As for me, the discovery of the rat destroyed the miracle. For a time I couldn't stop thinking that behind every mystery for mankind there's always a rat hiding who will leap out. The mystery disappeared and the rat appeared and it wasn't hard for me to discover why from the very first moment I felt myself in the same situation that it was in. The rat's an animal that's put upon. The rat's like me. In the zoology of society my solidarity with the rat comes from the fact that the rat is also a persecuted creature. We've got a hidden link. We belong to the race of those who run away, the band of those who fall into traps, or the species of those who are hunted, the family of those who have no right to live.

I get up as soon as the rat disappears. It must be quite early because there's no light and you can't perceive the usual movement in the jail during the first hours of daylight. I put my foot into the shoe and a small section of the inside still feels warm. It doesn't bother me, even though Braulio says that rats are infectious, like a leper's dog. That leads me to think that there's something that makes the existence of the rat stand out for me with peculiar characteristics.

During the day I wear my shoes. Shoes are meant to be worn on the feet. I'm not concerned with them. During the day my shoes don't exist for me because they're a part of me.

But Braulio Coral's shoes also exist as he spends the first part of the morning and the last hour of evening cleaning them. He polishes them tirelessly until they gleam in his hands, glowing in the darkness. What's surprising is that he doesn't clean them to wear. He ordinarily puts on some rope sandals and that's how he goes through the day until at night, worn out from polishing shoes, he also divests himself of the sandals.

It's never occurred to the rat to choose Braulio's hygienic shoes over my dirty ones. Maybe the proletarian neglect that makes them look like garbage is precisely what he likes most about mine. In any case, he never lodges in the shoes of Braulio Coral, who places them in a certain way near mine, perhaps with the unconfessed hope that the rat will fill them someday with the heat of his body and his night.

I venture to say that the rat's disdain is a great humiliation for Braulio Coral. For him shoes are the physical mechanism of freedom. They're the leather track that will take him one day, like a train, out of the station that is the jail. He polishes them frantically, as if he were trying to give freedom a shine through them. Braulio can't forgive the rat the disdain it shows for his gleaming shoes.

SATURDAY, OCTOBER 17

Eleven more hours until the changing of the guard.
He was going to live his longest night, the night without end.
　Emmanuel Robles

The pencil has been worn down so much that I've begun to write with my fingernail too. Luckily, David loaned me a fountain pen yesterday afternoon with the proviso that I don't write too much. So until I get another pencil I'll have to be brief.

At dawn I find myself once more in the corner where a frustrated attempt at a wall has made room there for the placement of a metal washstand and the chamber pots. In the cell the other three are still sleeping. Although a barred window that opens onto the main courtyard prevents any excessive accumulation of the stench of our sleep, in the cell we breathe the hundred thousand atmospheres of the depths of the earth discussed by geophysics. Nevertheless, in a certain way this cell doesn't make for a crushing atmosphere of misfortune like those dungeons I saw with my own eyes in another jail that I visited many times, not as a prisoner, but as the son of the warden, its tyrant.

The first thing I do after washing my face is to water the rosebush. We call it that, but the rosebush consists of a rose that's always alive because, as an artificial rose, it's destined to take a long time to die. I never found out how the rose got into the prison. The only sure thing was that it got there and as a tribute to the beauty of the world we resolved to keep it in the cell. In any case, as something spurious it was an appropriate flower for the greenhouse atmosphere of the jail.

It occurred to Braulio Coral later on that we should plant it. We put a little soil into a clay cup and there we stuck the wire that imitates the stem of the rose.

It stands gracefully over the handful of earth, but unfortunately when there's a furtive little gust of wind, as when someone passes close to the flower, it rustles, as though trying to remind us that instead of being a rose it's nothing but a miserable little paper decoration. Its planting necessarily brought with it the next technical step, which was its care and cultivation. Continuing the botanical buffoonery, I've ended up watering it every day. It's a job that calls for hydraulic horticultural skills. One clumsy drop could dissolve it.

David Fresno can't accept this madness, but what's certain is that this madness has succeeded in establishing itself in the cell. The only time the subject came up was the day David said to me:

"Don't expect the rose to perfume the cell. It would be like expecting a porcelain cow to give you milk."

"Flowers don't just serve to give off a scent," Braulio observed with the calm assurance of a housewife.

"Antón should have grown some marijuana instead of cultivating roses," Mister Alba said.

Braulio smiled. Braulio smiles a lot because he almost always agrees with the others.

"That's right. Marijuana would find a homey climate for growth in here."

16

David interposed himself again:

"Flowers mean something different for everybody. For Antón Castán they're poetry. For bees they're honey."

Mister Alba lent a hand:

"For asthmatics flowers are toxic."

"For a woman they're a beautifier," David went on. "For a dead person they're a last wish. An Italian naturalist said that flowers are a plant's menstruation. I suppose for a French industrialist involved in the perfume business flowers are an underdeveloped scent."

I decided to join the game too.

"Out of all of them," I stated, "only the gardener is right. For a gardener a flower is just a flower."

David returned to the attack:

"I should like to know the reason you're cultivating a rose that can't be cultivated."

"He most likely wants to wear it in his buttonhole the day he goes free," Mister Alba said.

"Or maybe he's keeping it to wear on Mother's Day. A dead flower for a dead mother," David added.

Since I didn't like their sullying the rose and didn't want them to humiliate me either, I felt hurt by David's words. If there's something that bothers me more than an insult it's a lack of awareness of the pain it causes me. I answered:

"You're wrong, David. I'm not cultivating it for myself. I water it so I'll be able to lay it on your coffin the day they take your corpse from this cell."

David hasn't brought up the rose since. I think he sees it as an epitaph, as though he could already feel it floating over his grave.

I water the rose, which is starting to grow old but which still bears itself proudly with its artificial veins, its dead sap, its desiccated petals the color of fake blood. Several drops of water remain quivering on the wire root for a moment. At that spot the earth seems to be rebelling against the fraud of our illusory cultivation.

Climbing onto the stack of books and magazines piled up in disorder beneath the window, I take a look through the bars. In the main sentry box across the way a guard is writing by the light of an oil lamp. Not even when he's writing does he let go of his submachine gun. Such weapon-like writing gives him a comical look. He has the ancient air of a militarized notary or a retired general absorbed in the writing of his memoirs.

A bed creaks behind me. Someone is stirring. Since his bed is next to mine I know that it's Braulio Coral who's restless in his.

Things happen the same way every day. First I get up. When I've made my obligatory inspection through the window, which is something like making sure that the outside world still exists, Braulio Coral also wakes up. Then the two of us start to chat.

That gives rise to the half-asleep Mister Alba dedicating himself to cursing in English. It also gives rise to David associating himself with Mister Alba's grunts but in a concrete and caustic Spanish bolstered by picturesque expressions. The one who always comes off the worst is Braulio Coral. His irrelevant comments serve David to remind him every morning, and in a not too benevolent way, that his custom of rising early comes from the time when Braulio plied the ambulant trade of a house painter in the streets of the city, starting at dawn with a ladder on his shoulder.

"What time is it?" Braulio asks.

"It's just starting to get light," I answer.

"Quiet, painter!" David yells.

Contrary to his custom, Braulio rolls over in bed and continues sleeping. I have no other recourse but to go back to bed myself. In the monotonous prison timetable, where the presence of a rat achieves the status of an essential

18

theme for meditation and a noticeable spiritual unrest, there's nothing so tedious as this. Getting up and having to go back to bed right after is the cruelest of tortures.

With no place for me to move to, unable to read in the half-light inside there, afraid of bothering my cellmates if I keep on chatting with Braulio Coral the painter, the only recourse left for me is trying to go back to sleep. Piling sleep on top of sleep until the rest makes my eyes puffy, until the lethargy gives me a headache, until the surfeit of sleep starts changing into an unhealthy insomnia. Gathering sleep into my head in order to be able to live in sleep's dark land. Going to bed at this hour after having a premonition of the world through the window is like burying myself in a grave deeper than death and almost as overwhelming as hell.

In jail, insomnia is sleep and sleep is agony. You're not asleep but you're not awake either. You're in that impenetrable region where crimes rest in the flesh of the man who is their prisoner. The terrible thing about jail isn't that it enslaves our bodies but that it crushes us with the mummifying weight of forced sleep, which most resembles the sleep of eternity.

In the Bible there's mention of a patriarch who "lived full of days." I live full of nights, lying in bed in the long jail night with my waking sleep.

When I was free, I could recall my life clearly. Since I've been in jail I can only dig about in the confused dung-hill of my dreams.

In jail it's not only men who sleep. In this pool of stagnant water, time sleeps too, like a fish caught on the hook of weariness and oblivion.

SUNDAY, OCTOBER 18

No human being is sufficiently good to be a jailer.
   Sinclair Lewis

I don't know why, but Mister Alba makes me think of my father.

My grandfather, who'd been a colonel in the Thousand Days War, wanted my father to follow a military career, but my father desisted when he realized that a military man is only good for war. A pacifist as the result of a lack of war during a period of provincial and civil peace, my father had to resign himself to being a modest municipal administrative functionary. As part of this service he was warden of a jail in a village lost in the highlands of the Colombian Andes. Seen from the surrounding mountains the dirty and vegetable yellow houses of the village gave an impression of kernels of corn scattered haphazardly into the valley between the heights.

I must have been eight at the time. For various reasons I used to go to the jail a lot to see my father. When I left school I preferred visiting the jail to going defenseless into the big lonely house where my mother, whom I'd never known, survived uselessly in a portrait.

In that way, ever since childhood and without wanting

20

to, I came in contact with a penal environment. I remember the jail my father ran was a gloomy one, inhabited by monstrous murderers who would appear in my young dreams. At least that was what I thought they were when in my father's office I came across those faces that seemed coated with blood, proclaiming the horror of their crime.

During that time the jail had been my true and only home in a certain way. I would hang around in the office for a while taking in the small discoveries of life while my father interrogated prisoners or gave orders to the guards. In the evening we would both go home, where he read the *Official Daily* while I did my homework. There was a small number of schoolmates who on exceptional occasions dared come to play with me in that house where the warden lived. For some reason they felt him to be a more or less benign extension of an executioner.

That house with a father who didn't pay much attention to me, that house where the servants humbled me with their servile indifference, that house with no mother or brothers and sisters oppressed and overwhelmed me. Jail today is nothing but a prolongation of it. As a prisoner I am continuing a family tradition except that instead of a prisoner I ought to be a warden like my father.

What made the house even more intolerable was the portrait where a young woman who didn't look like a mother but a frustrated virgin kept following me wherever I might be with her stiff eyes that had been touched up with oil. The painter had succeeded in giving those eyes a gleam that had the task of interrogating and watching over me.

The figure in the picture was even less attractive when I thought of how she was linked to certain imprudent words on the part of my father. Words that put me into a spiritual confusion, which I have never been able to fathom as I should have. One day, looking at the portrait, my father told me in a grotesquely solemn tone that my mother had been a saint. That classification made an unfavorable impression on me. As an infantile sinner I didn't feel too comfortable as the unworthy son of a saint. The shame was made worse later on when a schoolmate talking about his own mother told me she was a saint. I heard that same concept many times after. Evidently, I said to myself in resignation, all us men are the sons of saints.

I remember quite well that the jail my father ran was governed by rules of a terrifying medieval severity. Prisoners whose conduct left something to be desired were put in the stocks, a leftover from Spanish punishment during the colonial period. There were also fetters, shackles, chains, and dungeons. Prisoners would remain weeks on end stuck between four asphyxiating walls that almost touched each other. The punishment of bread and water once a day also for weeks on end was common. To perfect the picture my father exercised his authority in the prison with resolute energy. A lot of people thought he exercised it with great cruelty.

I don't have available, however, any complete information with which to judge my father's conduct as warden. After all, my father was my father and his justice was the justice of his time. On the emotional level I grew closer to my father with feelings of affection, gratitude and respect that have never disappeared completely. Quite the contrary, they have been affirmed and purified since he left this world, leaving behind his house adorned with countless swords from my grandfather and loaded down with accumulated mortgages that turned out to be much more cutting than the swords. When the judicial processes began the family inheritance fell to pieces. Creditors divided up the house room by room. All I had left were the swords from a war that wasn't mine.

In the jail my father ran I found a small book whose author was the magistrate Francisco Bruno. Its title was *The Comedy of Justice*. Regarding that book, only later did I read something similar concerning the slow-moving action of justice in the labyrinths of *The Trial*, by Kafka, and in the moth-eaten files of *Corruption in the Palace of Justice*, by Ugo Betti.

I enjoy recalling the book by Magistrate Bruno, who was certainly not a magistrate when he wrote it, because of the arbitrary outline of a fable it inspired in me. This fable, however, is more or less faithful to *The Comedy of Justice*.

A man is waiting in jail for a judge's decision.

During the first month the inexperienced judge doesn't dare make a decision because he doesn't know how. During the second month the judge is quite busy examining the charges against other prisoners whose cases are more urgent or more important. During the third month the judge is away from his post because of strictly confidential family matters. During the fourth month a sister of the judge's loses her honor, which leads the equable judge to abstain from judging because he himself has lost his equanimity. During the fifth month the judge spends his time complaining to the government for not having paid his salary and for having paid him poorly. On the sixth month the imploring and rebellious judge is discharged for incompetence. On the seventh month, when the prisoner has lost all hope, he is consoled by the news that the judge is a prisoner along with him in the same jail.

That's the lesson of *The Comedy of Justice*, more or less.

Of course, on arriving at this real jail where I find myself, I learn certain procedures of humanitarian justice are beginning to be established in the nation's penal system. There are no shackles, chains, dungeons, or whipping posts here. There's no death by degrees, that is, hunger with the evangelical rations of bread and water. In some sense there's a certain comfort that can be enjoyed here. If you're lucky enough not to be locked up in the common dormitories, huge halls with heaps of human manure, inhuman blood sausages stuffed with jail meat, imprisonment can be less cruel. If, in addition, you've got a little money, you can buy other additional advantages according to the rules or by irregular means.

Mister Alba doesn't complain. Talking to me about these things he says,

"Here at least you don't lose your head."

"I don't know, a lot of prisoners go crazy," I tell him.

"I'm not referring to that," Mister Alba explains. "What I meant was that here at least you survive. They locked up John the Baptist in a cistern and along with that they cut off his head."

MONDAY, OCTOBER 19

You can't go to heaven if the freedom to go to hell doesn't exist.
    Salvador De Madariaga

Braulio Coral has started to sneeze. He sneezes once, then fifty times. He does it in comical spasms, wiping his nose after each one and tightening his face in expectation of the coming seizure. Looking at him, David starts to laugh.

"I see you've caught cold," he says.

"I don't think so," Mister Alba states.

"Why?"

"It's too much. It must be a case of some allergy."

"But why can't it be a cold?"

"A cold presupposes a draft, a current of fresh air. You can't tell me that Braulio's been exposed to that here."

"According to Mister Alba prisoners like us haven't got the right to catch ourselves a cold," David says.

"We haven't," Mister Alba assures him. "A cold is an illness of free men. In this damp and stinking hole all we can hope for is rheumatism. Rheumatism is the typical illness of prisoners. If it weren't for jails the medical profession would never have been aware of the existence of rheumatism."

"Do you suffer from rheumatism, Mister Alba?" I ask.

"No. I'm one of the few old prisoners who haven't come to know rheumatism here. I'm an exceptional prisoner as far as rheumatism is concerned. Life has given me the opportunity to be extraordinary in some way."

Mister Alba thinks he's an extraordinary being because he hasn't come down with rheumatism in jail. By the same criterion Socrates could have called the act that took away his shackles happiness.

Mister Alba divides the world into two parts: what belongs to the jail and what's outside it. The same conclusion that he's just drawn from Braulio's sneezing he applies to all concepts of life, which for him either are or aren't a part of jail. He continues:

"I've only seen sneezing like that which goes on for a hundred times without stopping coming from a dead man. He was in the same cell with me. All of a sudden he dropped dead and after he was dead he started to sneeze without stopping. Some mechanism for a separate action must have been left alive in his organism that was unaware of his death and kept on functioning afterwards, like the spring of a watch that's been smashed to pieces or like the crazy wheel that keeps on spinning on a car that's gone over a cliff. It's funny how a man isn't surprised by a terrible everyday thing like death and on the other hand is upset by an unexpected foolish thing like the sneeze of a dead man. I wasn't scared by the man who'd died, I was scared by the man who started sneezing after he was dead."

Regarding the dead man who sneezed after he was dead, in the jail my father ran I once saw something that I can't forget. It was a prisoner who after he was dead and buried continued to be a prisoner.

In the jail my father ran an inmate had died with his leg irons on. If the sentence to wear irons was a long one, for the convenience of officials the lock was removed and a blacksmith would weld the irons together so that the punishment would be even heavier psychologically for the soul of the prisoner. In the case of this man something had to be done because the corpse was beginning to decompose.

Prisoners don't last very long when they're dead. The very irons had begun to smell like rotted metal, dead iron. A purple fly (that's the color flies wear to smell dead people) was leaping greedily around the irons and the feet.

Since the blacksmith, who was a drunkard, was nowhere to be found, my father decided to bury the man with his irons in place. There was nothing else to be done. I watched when they took him out. He was on a stretcher, tied to the rods as though they were still afraid of his escaping, and covered with a sheet that didn't reach down to cover his feet. I've never seen a prisoner imprisoned so atrociously as that dead man. It was as though he'd been sentenced twice over: held between the rings of iron and a prisoner in the clutches of death.

When they carried out the corpse something horrible occurred to me. I don't know why, but I was sure that with those irons on the dead man wouldn't be able to get into heaven. In heaven, I thought, there can't be any men in irons. The prisoner, therefore, was marked for hell and what tormented me most was the fact that the fires of hell would turn the irons on the condemned man's feet red-hot.

My father's cold bureaucratic sense of scruples led him to say, "I've got to account for the disappearance of the irons, which have got to figure in the inventory of items in the jail."

"Don't worry," my father's secretary answered. "It'll be easy to account for the disappearance of the irons."

"How?"

"We'll say the dead man stole them. After all, he did carry them off."

My father authorized him to do just that. And thus in the jail's inventory of supplies in which a man can be missing but not a set of irons, the posthumous accusatory evidence was registered that the dead man was a thief because he'd carried the irons off to the grave.

I can't say what the obsequious secretary's name was, but I can recall, one might say even audibly, his manner of speaking. His speech wasn't anything solid, like the speech of men. His voice had a wetness about it and the words came out from between his lips like bubbles. His voice was something liquid, like a woman's weeping.

I can't remember his name. He was a thoroughgoing underling and an exemplary jailer. It wasn't his real tongue but his adulatory saliva that spoke in him.

TUESDAY, OCTOBER 20

I hate victims, most of all because they oblige me to kill them.
Giovanni Papini

It's still quite early when Braulio starts hounding Mister Alba. Without saying anything he follows him with his eyes and scrutinizes him insistently.

"When you start looking at me that way," Mister Alba says, "it's because you want something from me. How much?"

"You hit it," Braulio answers. "I need your help."

"How much?"

"A hundred pesos."

"That's a lot of money. I can let you have seventy."

"I need the hundred."

"Go get them somewhere else. I can only lend you seventy and for that I'll need a guarantee."

"I was aware of that."

"All I would've needed was for you not to be. Money isn't quoted at par in jail. It has one price for the one taking the risk and another for the one who gets the benefit."

Mister Alba takes from his pocket his personal file, which is a pack of old papers, and draws seven ten-peso notes from it.

"It's all I've got," he explains. "What's your guarantee?"

"I don't know. How about a ring?" Braulio answers.   "How about a wedding ring?"

"From which of your weddings would you mind telling me?"

Braulio smiles. He must be thinking about his two wives. Mister Alba continues:

"In any case, you know already. I don't take anything gold as a pledge. Gold has the quality of demoralizing me. It inspires ideas of escape in me. I went off the gold standard a long time ago."

"I could give you my shoes," Braulio implores him.

"Not even with the ring inside could your shoes be worth seventy pesos."

"The Christ, then."

Braulio takes the silver Christ out of his pocket. It's obvious that it would be a great effort for him to give it up.

Mister Alba rejects it. The same thing always happens. When he's set to do a favor he argues, haggles, lays down all sorts of conditions, but at the last moment he ends up dropping them and doing the favor with a generosity that at least for his cellmates is always limitless. Mister Alba likes the play-acting that precedes the loan, not the profit that comes after.

"All right," he concludes. "If the Christ is all you've got, keep it. I'll make sure you pay me later."

That's not true either. Mister Alba never gets back what he lends.

Braulio puts the Christ and the seventy pesos away. The anxious face that had pursued Mister Alba before is filled with serene happiness now.

"What do you need the money for?" I ask him.

"To split between his wives," David says, with a loud laugh.

This scene of the frustrated contract for the Christ brings back to my memory another Christ in another jail. Behind the desk where my father worked hung an ivory Christ. It was a beautiful piece, without much artistic value but loaded with a moving spiritual allegory.

It's very hard for me to get the memory of the Christ in that office out of my head. There's a detail in my memory that won't let me forget it. Underneath the Christ was an oak chest, a piece of antique furniture that I'd never paid much attention to. One day when my father wasn't present I was suddenly seized with curiosity to open the chest. I opened it and it was full of irons, rusted metal still stained with the blood of the feet that had suffered in them. Before my eyes the blood of the irons suddenly rose up to the blood on the brow of Christ and those two bloods came together for me into the single bloody flood of pain. That phenomenon, while it purified my admiration for Christ, at the same time left me pierced through with the horror of the irons.

Because of the obsession that followed that hallucination and not out of any fear of being put in irons, but rather of being put in the infamous position of having to put them on someone in childhood games, I could never play the role of a policeman. Later on I refused to wear rings on my fingers. I like my hands of a man to be naked of those rings of submission that are irons in their golden phase. Even religious medals and their allegories frighten me with a sacred fear, because their tinkle and glimmer remind me of chains.

I've meditated a lot about that figure of Christ in relation to the jail here.

It's strange but instructive that the symbol of Christianity is a symbol of torture, that is, an instrument of imprisonment. Until the Mount of Olives, Jesus appears as the shining apostle of universal charity. He must be taken prisoner, receive unjust punishment, be sacrificed on the cross, and converted into a victim for his condition as redeemer of humankind to be finally consolidated. I think it's this consubstantiation of man and cross that changes prisoners into creatures beloved of the Lord. I think this is the link that brings cross and jail together.

The idea of jail was by no means alien to the teachings of Christ. He defined jail quite well when he said that on the day men fall silent the stones will cry out. Prisoners are the men who are silent; jail the stones that cry out.

In my father's office Christ is writhing in pain in that ivory incarnation and it was impossible to think under the pressure from the shudder that his martyrdom aroused how that image there could be taken for the visible manifestation of divine pity. It took me a long time to discover why.

The reason lay in the fact that Christ had no escape, encrusted in the ivory, yoked to the cross. The reason was that Christ's tormented face was changed for me into the face of human torture. One day I finally saw it all quite clearly. In Christ, God was prisoner. The discovery filled me with terror but at the same time it filled me with serene confidence in the truth. Ever since, Christ for me has represented the figure of all men who are prisoners. For a long time this irreverent yet purifying relationship has touched me.

All these associations are the ones that have led me to think afterward about what Christ means. Christ means that a prisoner is not alone. In the spiritual order Christ means for me that I'm strong. With him we're two. In jail, however, I continue seeing him dying; I continue seeing him imprisoned. Christ is a prisoner because he's with me.

32

WEDNESDAY, OCTOBER 21

It is preferable for ninety-nine guilty people to go free than
for one innocent person to be punished.
  Bertrand Russell

A guard has come for Braulio. Braulio runs to the washstand and starts combing his hair.

It's a bit grotesque to see him combing his hair when
he has several days' growth of beard and is wearing his
inevitable rope sandals, ragged pants, and a grimy shirt.
In spite of being framed like that, a manly face gleams
over his robust body, animated at this moment by the ir-
repressible joy of sensing that in just a short while his
nostrils will stop breathing the nauseating air of the cell.

Braulio's sloppy look is in sharp contrast to the
decorous and tidy appearance of Mister Alba. The latter
always wears a tie and never takes off his jacket. He says
that he can live without pants but never without a jacket.
And he never takes off his hat, which he only removes
when it's time for bed.

"I'm a gentleman," he said one day, using the English
word. "A gentleman must always be well-dressed, even in
his own home."

"Who told you this is your home?" David asks.

"And who said it isn't?"

"Pardon me, I thought this was a jail."

"It is a jail, but it's been my home from the moment it gave me shelter and from the moment I started living in it."

"Well, anyway, I never heard of gentlemen wearing their hats in the house."

"Gentlemen wear hats wherever they feel like wearing them. That's why they're gentlemen."

Mister Alba always wears a medal on the lapel of his jacket. He says he got it from the government of Colombia for distinguished service in the war with Peru. He also states that it was in that war, in the Amazon region, where he lost the eye he's missing. When he talks about the missing eye he does so with an accent that's a mixture of the resentment of a mutilated person and the pride of a decorated one.

I must report some more things about Braulio. Of all of us he's the only one who prays in the morning when he gets up. He does it on his knees with the silver Christ in his hand, looking up at the ceiling where he himself has painted some silver stars. Every chance he gets Braulio paints silver stars there in order to create the illusion at night that he's free to look at the sky. In contrast to Mister Alba, who sleeps in silk pajamas, or to David and me who sleep in cotton ones, Braulio sleeps in his shorts, which never ceases to shock Mister Alba. While Braulio continues combing his hair, Mister Alba tells him:

"Don't work on your hair so much. The heads of prisoners who are going to be hanged look better uncombed."

That sort of graveyard humor is quite common among us.

In order to erase the impression that the joke has made on Braulio, I ask the guard:

"I'm in urgent need of pencils and paper."

"How much paper?" the guard asks.

"All you can get me."

"Give me the money."

"I haven't got any right now, but if you bring me some pencils and paper I'll pay you whatever you ask."

"Are you going to write an appeal to the president for clemency?" the guard asks.

"Has the president got any clemency available?" Mister Alba asks in turn.

"Don't bad mouth the president," David says. "If he wants to have fun, let him do it with his ministers. That's what ministers are for."

"Seriously, is he writing to the president?" the guard asks again.

Mister Alba has his say once more:

"No, guard. He's writing the history of the jail."

"If that's the case I'll bring you some pencils and paper," the guard says agreeably.

That's enough to make me forget the bad humor the guard showed before when I'd asked him to sharpen my pencil.

"For Christ's sake bring him what he wants," David demands from his corner. "I want to keep my fountain pen in shape."

After the guard has taken Braulio away we all sit there in silence. Six eyes are impatiently on watch in the shadows. Every time one of the four of us goes out there's an exceptional opening for the three left. If one leaves it's a chance for the other three to talk freely about him.

When the four of us are together we form the unbreakable blockade of an enigma. With one gone the curtain rises for its revelation. These four men stuck together and yet absent are four strangers to each other in spite of the fact that they're always there, that they eat together, sleep together. Every day the four of us become even greater strangers to one another. We're four people caged up in our secrets.

"What do you think the judge is going to tell him?"

"He'll give him a lecture on the Penal Code and send him back here."

David's voice is hard when he says that.

"I wonder who drew up the Penal Code?" Mister Alba asks.

"People I know think it comes down from the Romans," David says. "The Romans were specialists in codes and since then the world has specialized in applying Roman codes. In this business of codes there's a continuation of Roman imperialism. Read our Penal Code, Mister Alba. From translation to translation, from assimilation to assimilation, from copy to copy our Penal Code is a code made to punish Romans. Our Penal Code seems to have been put together to give Nero a scare."

"I can't waste my time," Mister Alba announces. "I've got enough self-respect left not to spend my time reading the Penal Code."

"I've read it," David states. "From end to end. It's a funny kind of document. It deals with everything except justice. Looking for justice in the Penal Code is like looking for humanity in the phone book."

It's conversations like this that Mister Alba can't resist joining in, with pompous and didactic authority.

"The lack of justice stems from the fact that the Penal Code is a statistical record of crimes that's been adulterated by the uprightness of men who haven't committed any. It's as though virgins were to write treatises on moral values in order to teach those who aren't virgins. Penal Codes should be written by prisoners."

I'm thinking about what David had said when Mister Alba asks me:

"Antón, have you read the Penal Code?"

I think a bit before answering. Finally I say something:

"Yes. Reading codes is good exercise for the brain. A writer could read the Penal Code in order to improve his style, but I read it in order to damage mine."

David seems enthusiastic with my answer.

"That leads me to believe that what you've been writing is pretty bad," Mister Alba says.

"Could you tell me, finally, what you have been writing?"

I look at David before answering.

"I'm writing a diary."

"An intimate one?" he asks.

"It's a diary of events."

"We've got newspapers for that."

"Newspapers have the disadvantage of being written in freedom. Newspapers aren't written in jail."

"Do I appear in the diary?"

As Mister Alba asks the question, there's a touch of anxiety in his voice.

"Yes, Mister Alba. You too are an event," I reply.

"Antón, do you think they'll release Braulio?" David asks me.

"That depends on the judge," I say.

"Not on the judge," David observes, "on the Code."

"Not on the Code," Mister Alba corrects, "on the bigamy."

David licks his lips.

"Bigamy. That's the only crime I envy Braulio for. Bigamy. A delicious crime, bigamy."

David hasn't spoken the last word when we hear the

footsteps of Braulio and the guard. A moment later he's in there with us.

"What did the judge say?"

"I didn't get to see him. He had to go out and pick up a dead body. He left word for me that he'll see me next week."

THURSDAY, OCTOBER 22

Freedom is the free man's prison.
  Lawrence Durrell

The guard has brought me the pencils and paper. I'll be able to write from now on not only without any restrictions, but also in comfort. The guard had added a pocket pencil sharpener to the request on his own. When I thank him for his services I ask him how much I owe him. He tells me:

"When they heard it was for a prisoner they refused to charge me anything."

"Who gets the thanks, then?"

"It's a gift to the jail. It's a gift from freedom."

The guard calls the jail *jail*. The rest of the world he calls freedom.

When the guard leaves we sit there discussing freedom. Each of us has formed a capricious concept of freedom made to the measure of his own inclinations or personal convenience. In jail each one of us drinks the magical brew of freedom with different lips.

For Braulio Coral, the vagabond wall painter, freedom consists of having a big brush.

39

For Mister Alba, the adventurer who collects post cards, freedom is reduced to an international passport.

For David Fresno, the bohemian student who landed in jail for posing as a relative in a bank fraud, freedom is a rubber check.

For me, a writer, but most of all because I'm innocent, freedom is something else.

Freedom means something different for every man. Running away from the humiliation of slavery, a man looks for freedom, chases it, enjoys it, understands it. The drama starts when there are two men, because two men can't agree anymore when they talk about it. Freedom is an enigma that's close at hand.

On the matter in question, Mister Alba gives us a flashy show of humanistic knowledge.

"Having heard so much talk about it, I sometimes think that freedom doesn't exist at all. Cervantes pointed out that freedom was a road. Hegel thought that freedom was a choice. Nietzsche proclaimed that freedom was a hierarchy. Clemenceau harangued that freedom was duty. Unamuno conjectured that freedom was chance. I think that while all of them were right, none of them was completely right. I've made the great discovery in this cell: freedom is jail."

Mister Alba is silent and for a moment the cell is filled with the warm presence of freedom. At first the freedom of the cell is like a dizzying sound: a sound forgotten by our heart that seems to be coming from far away. Then it takes the form of an unexpected wind whose caress excites and dazzles us, as though a ball of sunlight had just fallen into our hands. Our eyes, overwhelmed by fear and baseness and darkness, are blinded for a moment by freedom. Then the freedom, noise, breeze, and light of prisoners begins to throb in our blood. Mister Alba is right. Freedom is here with us.

In order to stanch this outpouring of erudition by Mister Alba, I allow myself the observation:

"For Epictetus, who was a philosopher, freedom was knowledge. For Freud, who was a dreamer, it was a dream. For D'Annunzio, who was a poet, freedom was victory. You could go on like that forever quoting thought after thought, right up to the infinite, the contradictory reactions of all men as they look upon freedom. In this way freedom is like an escalator which, step by step, never passes because it never stops passing."

I fall silent, but I don't stop thinking about freedom. The sum total of all these isolated preferences, the accumulated exactitude of all these divergent definitions still, in some way, shed light on and complement each other and it leads me to a shocking conclusion: freedom is nothing because freedom is everything.

In other words, freedom is life.

But it can also be death. Diogenes the Cynic preached that freedom is death.

FRIDAY, OCTOBER 23

If Dreyfus is not innocent, let it all come tumbling down!
  Émile Zola

When we go near the cell door we realize that the guard is armed with an assault rifle.

"What's that toy for?" David asks him.

"For prisoners who want to be heroes," the guard replies.

"Seriously. Why are you carrying a rifle instead of a revolver?"

"Don't worry, I'm carrying a revolver, too."

"And a knife?"

"Not a knife, a bayonet. It's new, never been tried out."

"It can't be said that you're unarmed."

"We do what we can."

"But what's going on? Why are you carrying a rifle? Something must be up since you're armed with a rifle."

"Bandits. They're in the hills not far from here. They attacked a post in the mountains and killed eleven police-men."

"Only eleven?" Mister Alba asks.

"Eleven. That's all there were at the post," the guard explains.

David observes:

"The cops are going to have to take refuge in jail. Jail's the only safe place in the country now."

The guard remains silent. He catches sight of me and stares. He's looking at me with eyes of armed hostility.

"If I'm not mistaken, you're Antonio Castán."

"I am."

"I came for you. I was forgetting."

"What about?"

"Your lawyer wants to see you."

"My lawyer?" I ask.

"His lawyer?" David asks.

The three men in the cell are hanging on my words. I don't know what to do or say. The guard explains:

"In any case, a man's looking for you. He says he's your lawyer."

"Antón doesn't have a lawyer," Mister Alba says.

"Since he doesn't have a judge, it's even more unlikely he'd have a lawyer," David adds.

The guard opens the door and I go out. I walk along the damp, dark corridor toward the main courtyard. Since I haven't been out of the cell for several days now, walking makes me dizzy. I don't feel too steady on my feet. I feel as if I'd just got out of bed after a long illness.

I find the small visitors' room empty. But a moment later a man who looks like a fragment of a man makes his appearance. The guard stays there by the door. He looks at us as if we were conspiring and cocks his rifle, ready, it would seem, to open fire on us.

"Antonio Castán?" the little man asks.

"That's my name."

"I've come to offer you my services as attorney."

All this seems so strange to me that I don't dare say anything.

"I'm a penologist," he continues.

And I say timidly:

"Who sent you?"

"I had a visit with the judge who was studying your case yesterday."

"The judge?"

"Yes, the judge. Why does that seem strange to you?"

"I didn't know that the Department of Justice had found a judge for me."

"The judge, who's just been named, called attention to your case. He says that there's been a lot of talk about you and that something's got to be done about your crime. According to what I understand, you maintain you're innocent."

"I don't maintain. It's more important than that. I am innocent."

"Did you know the girl?"

"What girl?"

"The one they found strangled."

Good God! I can't hold myself back. I start laughing until the tears come. I laugh so convulsively that the lawyer starts showing surprise.

"You mean to tell me you didn't know?" he stammers.

"No, I didn't. It's only just now that I've found out why they're holding me prisoner. And I've got three years of jail behind me."

"Three years?"

"Yes. It's so painful when I tell myself that I almost can't believe it when I tell other people."

"It's incredible that something like this could have happened."

"That occurred to me too. At first I fought, made demands, threatened. Nobody would listen to me. I had to resign myself, in spite of the fact that some newspapers demanded justice for me."

"Do you swear that you're innocent? I've got to know. I couldn't save you any other way. Do you swear?"

"I don't swear anything. It's something more important than that. I am innocent."

It's funny. For the first time I was overcome at that moment by an unexpected feeling. For the first time I feel ashamed when I say I'm innocent. But I can't take back my words now.

One day, when we were talking about women in the cell, I got up the nerve to say that I'd never had a woman. They all looked at me with surprise. Men know that women are what make them men. At my age, in my time, in my country it was close to treason against the male gender. And yet I felt proud after I'd let it out. That was the last time I felt innocent before men.

Today I don't feel any pride in saying I'm innocent. When I say it my mouth fills up with a strange feeling, as if my teeth had bitten my tongue and the blood was flooding my saliva with fire.

At the same time, the crime I hadn't committed hurts me. I begin to feel something like a sort of criminal remorse for not having killed her and, of course, a kind of innocent nostalgia for not having known her.

The lawyer stares at me. He's disconcerted. He's begun to sweat and he takes out his handkerchief to wipe himself. He's so confused that instead of mopping his brow, which is dripping, he cleans his glasses, which are quite clean.

But I realize that he believes me. I realize that this unknown man has sensed my honesty and that his nostrils, free of the odor of evil, have caught the smell of my innocence. Neither he nor I can fool each other. The lawyer outlines his last doubt:

"You recognized your crime. At the police station you signed the document that attests to it. It's all in writing: you confessed."

"I didn't know what I was signing in the police station. They'd beaten me a lot. They didn't let me read what I'd signed. Still I had to do what they wanted. Make no mistake. We never write anything so clearly as when we have to sign our name with the barrel of a revolver stuck in our ear."

"That's all I needed," he declares quite firmly. "I'm going to defend you. I'll get you out of jail."

For a moment I can't say anything. It's the first time in three years that I've found any glimmer of human solidarity.

I tell him:

"I want you to understand that I'm not going against the judge. I'm only asking for the right to be heard before a judge."

"I understand," he replies. "It's not a matter of a mistake of justice here. It's a much simpler matter. It's matter of there being no justice."

"What's your name, Mr.....?" I ask.

"Not mister, doctor. Doctor of Law and Political and Social Sciences. I didn't spend five years at the National University to have someone call me mister as though I were a thief or a Deputy in Congress. My name is Antonio Ramírez. Doctor, please note, Doctor Antonio Ramírez."

He leaves without saying goodbye, without looking at me. I think for a moment that maybe he was really annoyed because I'd called him mister. But the face of the guard standing by the door gives me to understand the truth. I can read in face that Ramírez, Doctor of Law and Political and Social Sciences, has gone away touched by the man he's left, the man with three years of prison behind him.

SATURDAY, OCTOBER 24

Leonardo would buy caged birds in the market in order
to give them back their freedom.
  Emil Ludwig

You don't measure time in jail. In jail you feel time, the
way you feel a pain. That's why I've got to free myself
from time.

Today my watch has died. I broke it myself. What would
I want with hours here? Along with the watch time has
died for me, too. I killed the watch because my captivity
was getting tired of that little machine for manufacturing
useless minutes. With the split of the atom now, what's
needed is for me to break up the instant. I think I've done
that by breaking my watch.

I'm writing the above when the guard's measured steps
approach the door.

"Mister Alba," the guard calls.

"What do you want?" he asks.

"The director wants to see you."

I stop writing, David stops reading, and we all look
at Mister Alba. There's an anxious moment. Mister Alba
replies:

"I haven't got any time for living today."

"What do you mean by that?" the guard asks.

"I mean that I've only got time for reading."

"What do you mean?" the guard repeats.

"Tell the director I can't receive him today."

"If that's how it is I'm leaving. But this business of not being able to receive the prison director is going to cost you plenty."

"If you'd rather, so it won't cost me plenty, tell him that I've gone out, then, or that you couldn't find me," Mister Alba says.

When we're alone I ask Mister Alba: "Why did you say that?"

"What?"

"That business about not being able to receive the director."

"It's true. Why did I say it? Maybe I said it because I've lived enough today. This morning I cut my toenails."

I think that Mister Alba is right in a certain sense. Today is one of those days when we sink into our reading like into a deep well.

There are writers who don't do the talking themselves. In their books the voice of a country expresses itself, the presence of a people can be caught. The representative writers of the United States aren't Hemingway or Faulkner. The first is too universal. The meridian of his genius reaches beyond the borders of the United States. He takes part in the Spanish Civil War, even roams about Paris in *A Moveable Feast*. For his part, Faulkner is too provincial. He lives closed up in a southern county where there are planters and slaves, colonels or blacks, never any average Americans, never any absolute Americans.

The writer for absolute Americans is Sinclair Lewis. *Babbitt* is the result of the most thoroughgoing blood test ever made of Americans. And *Main Street*, although the street of one town, is the most complete literary picture of American urban gigantism. Lewis's world is the world of satiated men aspiring to be millionaires. Lewis's hunters after the dollar don't know what to buy with their freedom.

Lewis also wrote frightening and beautiful pages about justice and injustice as those concepts apply to the American milieu. Concerning the extent of justice, Lewis maintains that the penal law of the United States consists of locking the barn door after the horse has been stolen. Concerning the arbitrary form of injustice, Lewis says that the mental exam for policemen in the United States requires them to weigh 190 pounds.

The Spain of a period that goes from the decadence following the loss of its American colonies up to its present national resurrection hasn't been expressed as well anywhere as in the books of Azorín.

Azorín loves the symbols of uselessness, insufficiency, insignificance. In agriculture he prefers the lentil; in humanity the orphan; in art the miniature; in zoology the flea; in man the unemployed; in culinary matters the crumb; in the nation the village. "Paris is Jeannette's small town," says Azorín.

Azorín is the apostle of a literature of resignation. Azorín sees life with the criterion of a beggar. "History is a succession of coins," says Azorín.

For Azorín the free man is a servant. Azorín's men are not prisoners, but they carry inside a chaplain who threatens them with hell and a jailer who measures their steps. Azorín's Don Juan doesn't have passion but pity. Azorín's virgins aren't women but angels devoured by Andalusian anemia. Azorín's travelers don't know where they're going. Azorín's characters sigh and dress in mourning. "I don't know why they sigh so much, these old women dressed in black," Azorín says.

Mister Alba told me one day:

"Azorín isn't a writer for readers. Azorín is a writer for collectors."

I'm reading, then, two absolutely different writers. Azorín and Lewis are something more than two peoples. They're two opposite poles. Yet both of them are quite close to us. They both represent the two great cultural influences that have shaped the personality of our jail.

Azorín's Spaniard who endures hunger and makes it meritorious and Lewis's American who takes bicarbonate of soda after stuffing himself with hot dogs and makes it a heroic deed are characters I see here every day. In jail, at every step I run into Azorín's Spaniards (like Braulio) who pray as they count their pennies and Lewis's Americans (like Mister Alba) who don't wash their hands so as not to get rid of the smell of the putrid ink of dollars from their fingers. Both writers have a more or less equal share in the personality of our beloved jail.

Spain and the United States are the two tips of the historic tongs holding us prisoner, clutching us. The two tips make a joint effort unnecessary since between the two of them one makes the other useless. Where American influence shakes us up, Spanish tradition inhibits us. Where Spanish idealism drives us, American utilitarianism squashes us. Where Spanish rebellion pushes us into revolt against the colonial law of the jail, authorities in the American style immobilize us with the fierce encirclement of police dogs. The tragedy of our beloved jail consists in our not having sufficient personality to shake off the inhibitions of these two parallel yokes. Between these two forces that are squeezing us with their embrace, we haven't got to the point of being ourselves.

After so much reading I won't be able to sleep tonight. In order to sleep tonight I'll have to whistle in the dark.

SUNDAY, OCTOBER 25

Not one minute of freedom in jail:
you have to eat defending every mouthful.

   Fyodor Dostyevsky

Our lunch has consisted of a cup of a mixture of water and cornmeal. In an attempt to deceive us, each cup contains three Lima beans and two pieces of bone where, with great difficulty, the rancid smell of lamb persists. Mister Alba, who is a polite man, calls this soup *pottage*. Braulio, who is a patriot and one who follows folklore, calls it *mazamorra*, a kind of corn stew.

In one of his books Dr. Gregorio Marañón gives us to understand that *mazamorra* came to America on one of those floating jails they call galleys. It got here on a galley the same as almost all our ancestors and it came from Europe the same as almost all our authentically national dishes. "With the crumbs from biscuits," Dr. Marañón says, "they made a miserable soup called *mazamorra*." The only thing they did here was to make it even more miserable by substituting corn for biscuit crumbs.

The word *mazamorra* derives from *mazmorra*, meaning dungeon, from which one can deduce that *mazamorra* is a soup for prisoners.

For dessert we had a cup of hot water and sugar, also enlivened, not with lamb bones but with lemon peels. David says that they put lemon in the sweet water to slow digestion so food will be retained in the stomach longer and hunger will be slower in returning.

After lunch David, Braulio, and I occupy our respective beds. We're going to take a rest from having been resting all morning. I ask Mister Alba:

"Aren't you going to take a siesta?"

"I never take a siesta when I haven't got anyone to take a siesta with."

For Mister Alba a siesta is evidently a sexual act.

No sooner are we lying down than Mister Alba starts telling us about his life in the Amazon region. It's fun to listen as his voice gets all filled up with lies. It's a relief to be able to get away from the cell by means of that voice. David listens with his eyes closed. Braulio contemplates his stars on the ceiling. I look at Mister Alba, whose medal also shines in the shadows of the cell like another star.

"After the war with Peru I settled in Leticia. It's a miserable but fine region. I worked along with a Peruvian, a guy named Aguirre, a cruel man who'd been a rubber gatherer. In stories about the Amazon there always has to be a cruel man who'd been a rubber gatherer. Aguirre and I worked for Mr. Johnson, an educated gringo, a little nutty, who was determined to live among the native population in order to prove his theory that the early Americans were Japanese. In reality, in one of those magazines they bring Antón I read three days ago that Dr. Tulia de Dross is right now studying the similarity between the pottery of Haniwa figures in Japan and the Quimbaya figures of Colombia. As I was saying, we operated mostly between Leticia and Tabatinga, that is, the region formed by Colombia's

Amazonic wedge and the farthest tip of the Brazilian sub-continent."

Mister Alba falls silent for a moment and then continues on with more vigor:

"There we got to know and had dealings with the Tolabo Indians. Take your hats off, gentlemen, because we're coming to the land of the Tolabo Indians."

Ceremonious, as though he were an actor, Mister Alba takes off his hat with the gesture of someone greeting the Indians from a distance.

"They're a peculiar people. They cut off the ears of their babies at birth, so it's a society of earless people. They say that they cut off children's ears so they'll be able to see. In the Tolabo language 'ear' means 'eye' and vice versa. These Indians know where their senses are located. But that's not the only conceptual change in Tolabo culture. For them peace is war, so the pernicious concept of heroism doesn't exist there. For them life is death so they don't know suffering. For them the idea of freedom as we understand it doesn't exist. Among the Tolabos only good men are condemned and since they're all good, they're all prisoners."

He puts his hat back on, coughs loudly, and continues talking.

"From what I could see and hear, the Tolabos listen with their eyes and see with their mutilated ears. The Tolabos are like mad people painted by Dalí. According to Aguirre, the cruel rubber man, it's a verbal and psychological transmutation of ears and eyes that's fostered the South American legend of a country of the blind, immortalized by Wells in one of his stories. Actually, what started that legend was the Tolabos, and there's a good reason for it, because a man who sees through his ears is a blind man. In any case, the Tolabos are a wonderful people, almost as fantastic as a story by Wells."

David has fallen asleep. Braulio has stopped looking at his stars. I'm following Mister Alba's mad fantasies without tiring.

"If you look at them there, if you do see them and don't try to imitate them and see them with your ears, the Tolabos are very advanced people. Mr. Johnson, who was from Alabama and acted as though he were still living in the time of the War of Secession, said the Tolabos seemed to have been educated by Yankees. Indeed, the Tolabos worship the intestine. None of that adoring the sun or that kneeling down to the moon. For them the intestine is the incarnation of divinity. When a Tolabo dies the high priests, who are witch doctors and surgeons, perform a kind of sacramental autopsy on the deceased. After the autopsy they bury the body. They keep the intestine, dissect it, embalm it, and place it on the altar. Their temples are mounds of calcified guts, pyramids of intestinal mummies. Those architectural and monumental mounds of putrefaction would be horrific cemeteries of ignoble remains were it not for the Tolabos, who look at traditional art with their ears and listen to religious rites with their eyes, so that they never see the one or hear the other."

After this Amazonic and socio-paleontological rigmarole, I start dropping off to sleep. But I realize that it's not because no one's listening to him that Mister Alba stops talking about the Tolabo Indians.

MONDAY, OCTOBER 26

In an enslaved society, the biggest slave is the tyrant.
  Julián Marías

In our second interview lawyer Ramírez has just assured me that I'll have my freedom back in a couple of weeks. I hope God's listening. I signed a brief addressed to the judge, which gives my Dr. Ramírez the broad and sufficient power to defend and represent me. Although the rules say visits must be limited to twenty minutes, the lawyer made arrangements to stay with me for more than an hour. He spent the whole hour listening to me tirelessly as I talked about my past life, which can be summed up as twenty-two years of youth and three years of jail.

When I get back to the cell the three prisoners interrogate me expectantly.

"Is it true?"

"It is. The lawyer confirmed it."

"Has he already been appointed?"

"He's already taken over. He'll be paying us a visit before too long."

"What else did the lawyer say?" Braulio asks.

"He told me a lot of things about Leloya that have to do with me."

"What else?"

"He confirmed what we already know. Under Leloya the jail's going to be subject to a tyranny it's never known before," I inform them.

"Why did they pick him?" Braulio asks.

"They say it's to reorganize the jail with modern methods."

"I'm familiar with that kind of reorganization," Mister Alba mutters. "I know Leloya. He's the kind of man who seems predestined to be a jailer. Without mincing words, he's got the vocation of a true executioner." He ceremoniously tips his hat in a courtly gesture that's habitual with him and continues speaking. "So, my lads, we can kiss our beloved jail goodbye. Starting today this prison has been changed into a tomb."

We all laugh but we know that Mister Alba is telling the truth. We all know what the new warden, Tomás Leloya, means for the way the jail is run. Until today the prison has enjoyed a benign regime that only changed a few weeks ago when, for disciplinary reasons and until a new order is issued, our daily visits to the courtyard were suspended.

Leloya is a retired military officer. He's known as Major Leloya. When he was in the Army he became famous many years ago for his activities in pursuit and reprisal against guerrilla fighters. Cold and pitiless in guerrilla warfare, he didn't act like an official keeper of the peace but like just another bandit. During that period one incredible deed made him famous throughout the country.

A band of rebels had overthrown the municipal government of a mountain town. They shot the mayor, all the policemen, and all civil servants. They ransacked the stores, burned the church, the town hall, and the homes of several landowners. They proclaimed the town to be an independent republic, a miniature state that was like a cornered criminal, nothing but an orgy of madness and pillaging.

When the police and soldiers under the command of Major Leloya got there, after chasing the guerrilla band out of town, the armed units sent to maintain order accused the victims of having been accomplices in the attack. Then they indiscriminately applied a purification treatment of blood and fire to the inhabitants of the village—old men, women, children. The ones who didn't die the first night from a bullet in the ear were found the next morning hanging from the trees on the square. For five days, as there were no more living people to shoot, every time Leloya passed those hanging people he emptied his pistol into them, reiterating his deep desire that those hated dead be good and dead.

This was the man who was coming to take charge of our jail.

"If only they'd let us go out into the courtyard again..." Braulio sighs.

"If I were you I'd forget the courtyard," David says.

"If I don't see the sun pretty soon I'm going to go crazy."

"Leloya's going to extinguish the sun with his pistol. With Leloya there won't be any more sun," Mister Alba says.

Some time later Braulio starts to shake. Mister Alba feels his forehead.

"This fellow's burning up," Mister Alba tells us.

"We better call the guard," David says, pounding on the cell door.

Braulio's fever keeps rising. It's a fever that throbs and smells as if a man made of fever is starting to grow on top of the man of flesh. Being near him, the three of us share a little in the hot breath of his skin, which is beginning to give the cell a slight touch of animal warmth. The temperature in the cell has suddenly grown warm and unhealthy, a little sticky, like when a sooth-sayer in her unventilated room burns hairs in a brazier.

It's details like this that don't allow for the slightest hint of intimacy in jail. Even though each one of us keeps his secrets, those secrets flow out of our pores like sweat. We four men in the cell have got our souls all smeared with the same grease of repugnant promiscuity. Our minds are soiled with the thoughts of the others. Our mouths have the same taste of what the others are eating. We're four worms condemned to gnaw on an ulcer that's not only held in common but is inexhaustible.

The guard takes a long time in coming, but he finally gets there and opens the outside metal peephole in the door.

"What's the matter here?"

"Braulio Coral's got a very high fever. He'll have to be taken to the infirmary."

"The infirmary's not in use."

"But he's got to be taken out of here," I suggest. "He needs a doctor."

"The infirmary, the chapel, the visitors' room, the offices, even the hallways are all filled."

"Why?" Mister Alba roars. "Is there a civil war going on?"

"Prisoners. More prisoners. Robbers, murderers, kidnap-pers, prisoners are crowding in. They don't know where to put any more."

"That shouldn't stop you from getting a doctor."

"I'll see what I can do. But I'm not promising anything. There's no way of getting anything done here since this mess started. So many prisoners have arrived that the jail's busting at its seams."

"Is it true there's a new director?" David asks.

"Yes, Colonel Leloya."

"He's a colonel?"

"A colonel, and one of the best."

"I didn't know that military men could keep on getting promoted after they'd retired," Mister Alba says.

The guard answers:

"All I can say is that from today on we're going to have someone in charge here. Well, I'll go for the doctor now."

He goes for the doctor but comes back a half hour later to tell us there isn't any doctor. In the meantime, luckily, Mister Alba had used his wits and taken two pills out of his hat. Like a magician, he'd taken off his hat, lifted up the hatband, removed two pills, and given them to Braulio.

"Swallow these," Mister Alba ordered.

A moment later, with the same speed with which it had come on, the fever began to recede. A flash of victory showed in the solitary pupil of Mister Alba's Cyclops eye.

After the guard has left, Braulio says:

"I feel better."

"Did you think you were going to die?" Mister Alba asks him.

"That would have made me very sad," David says. "When a prisoner like Braulio decides to die, it's like someone dying a double death. It's no small thing to leave two widows behind."

TUESDAY, OCTOBER 27

I'm only free when I feel free.
Paul Valery

The morning has gone by and Braulio's fever hasn't come back.

"It's all thanks to your aspirin tablets," I tell Mister Alba.

"They weren't aspirin," he answers.

"What were they then?"

"Cocaine in pill form. It's the best thing for malaria."

"Who in the devil told you that Braulio's got malaria?"

"It doesn't matter. In any case he was cured by the pills, which weren't cocaine either."

The guard announces to Braulio that the judge wants to see him right away.

As they leave the guard stops him and puts handcuffs on him.

"Why are you putting handcuffs on him?" Mister Alba shouts.

"Those are my orders."

"That's a provocation," Mister Alba says, just to say something.

"I imagine it's just a precautionary measure," the guard says. "The jail's full. Prisoners and more prisoners. There

60

are a thousand prisoners in a jail built for four hundred. There's already talk of protests and riots."

After Braulio has left with his hands shackled, Mister Alba and David discuss it.

"I've never seen abuses like that anywhere," Mister Alba states.

"I have," David says. "That's what jails are for. By the way, Mister Alba, what are the jails in Panama like?"

"All I know about Panama is the canal, where I worked for three years. That's where I stopped being Señor Alba and changed into Mister Alba. That's where I learned English."

"You should have confessed that it was there you forgot your Spanish."

To change the subject, Mister Alba gets back to Braulio.

"I don't think that poor devil is any bigamist," he says.

"Don't badmouth Braulio, Mister One-Eye. He's your friend, after all."

Mister Alba gets furious when David calls him One-Eye, yet today he doesn't show any signs of wanting to object.

"He's my friend, that's true, but you ought to know that I only badmouth my friends. I prefer not talking about my enemies."

"Out of prudence?"

"No. Out of fear."

"Are you a coward, Mister Alba?"

"I suffer from 'buck fever,' which is what Theodore Roosevelt called the urge to run. I underwent treatment for cowardice, but I wasn't cured. It was in the Amazon region. In order to boost their courage and march off to peace, which is what they call war, the Tolabo Indians eat cheese made from bitches' milk. I ate that swill, but, frankly, after tasting it I was worse than before. I think they were fooling me. I think what they gave me was the white of a dove's egg."

"Why do you say that Braulio isn't a bigamist?" I ask.

"Because of his age," Mister Alba answers.

"His age?"

"Yes. Braulio's reached the age of men who can only allow themselves the luxury of being faithful."

"Explain yourself," David demands.

"I mean that bigamy isn't any sport for the old. And Braulio is already old. My contemporaries are beginning to grow old."

Before we can point out that Braulio is much younger than he, and as if to corroborate the idea that in spite of his contemporaries he's still young, Mister Alba begins to disassemble, piece by piece, the complicated external mechanism of his individuality. He takes off his jacket, takes off his shirt, takes off his undershirt. Then he opens the fold of skin where he keeps the tattoo and takes that out, too. He puts everything on the bed except the tattoo. He places the barber's razor in my hands.

When he's naked from the waist up, Mister Alba starts to do gymnastics. I look at him and I'm touched when I think of all that this ingenious and prevaricating man means to the occupants of the cell. I look at David, too, who must be thinking something similar. Many times he and I catch in each other's eyes that furtive glimmer that joins two men together in the same wordless secret.

"What would happen to freedom without jail?" David asks.

"What would happen to jail without freedom?" I point out.

Mister Alba interrupts his calisthenics. He takes a deep breath, ready to join in, and he joins in.

"The worst part is that jail is here and freedom is outside."

"No, Mister Alba," David says. "I can't accept that I'm a prisoner and that my freedom goes free."

Mister Alba won't concede defeat.

"Master Vargas Vila says that you can chain up a greyhound but not his howl. I say that when they cage a tiger they don't lock up in the cage the landscape he uses to kill."

"That means for you freedom is an accident of terrain," David says.

I come to his aid:

"What David's saying is true. How can freedom be separated from me? I'm in jail but my freedom hasn't abandoned me. My body and my soul make up my freedom and they're joined together and are with me."

After seven debilitating minutes of gymnastics, four of which he spent talking, Mister Alba rests. With great calm he begins to put back on the artful riddle of his external figure. The first thing he does is to tuck the tattoo back into the sheath he has in his belly.

WEDNESDAY, OCTOBER 28

It must be very hard to shoot a man who is laughing.
To kill you have to feel very important.
   Graham Greene

As I begin to write my hand copies down this thought, which has just come back to me. This automatic transcription gives me an idea. From now on I'm going to start my daily report with a sentence that has nothing to do with my worries of the day, just so long as it has to do with justice or jail. I've got a good supply of them collected from the books I've read over three years. This companionship with men who in some way have shared my anxiety for freedom will give me the incentive to keep going.

Naturally, this order I've imposed on myself will also get me to turn back. I'll cull out a few ideas from other people as headings for the daily chapters that have been written already.

I remember Graham Greene's phrase because Antonio Ramírez, Doctor of Law and Political and Social Sciences, my legal confidant whom I see almost every day now, told me two days ago that there's been talk lately of establishing the death penalty in the country. Some institutions and no few sociologists and lawyers are in favor of applying the death penalty to guerrilla fighters, gangsters, and kidnappers.

Every time a horrible crime is committed people think of the death penalty. Every time the aqueduct of public order that supplies us with the water of social peace gets clogged, people start to feel a thirst for blood. Criminal blood brings on a thirst for official blood. One murderer opens the way for another. We haven't got anywhere with a prison culture and now we're looking for a gallows civilization.

While the prisoners outside are discussing ways of setting up the apparatus of death, we prisoners here inside are suffering something worse because we've been condemned to the sterilizing punishment of living without living. I can't see why free men are so scandalized by the death penalty, which for someone in prison is an instantaneous relief, and yet remain indifferent to prison, which is a corrupting torture injected pore by pore, minute by minute, in slow motion with that most miserable little medicine dropper of human degradation.

As for capital punishment, Mister Alba tells me:

"In recent world history there have been two laughable examples of the death penalty. One is Nuremberg. The men hanged at Nuremberg are the posthumous cancer of the dead of the Second World War. The other is Israel. In the Eichmann case Israel dug out a whole mine of vengeance with incomprehensible refinements. The Eichmann case shows that for the first time in history the Jews didn't collect high interest since they were content with a transaction of the life of six million dead for the life of one man. Six million dead are not worth the murder of a murderer."

Whatever Mr. Alba says, people give too much importance to the death penalty. They go through centuries sanctifying or condemning it. They haven't realized that with it or without it, man will always be the same as long as this anteroom to death, which is jail, exists. People have made the death penalty into an immoral myth. This deformation has its origins in the customary monstrosity of applying a criterion that comes from the exercise of freedom to the phenomenon of punitive organization.

A free man looks with horror at the death penalty, even though he's its father. For the same reason a prisoner looks with horror at the law because he's its child. With an identical link but from a different position, the prisoner and the free man are accomplices in the fear of freedom. The vicious circle that makes a death penalty out of prison reaches the point of converting the death penalty into freedom.

If a free man knew that the death penalty isn't the worst thing, since it's just one punishment more going down one more corridor of humiliation and leading to one more cell, he'd stop talking about it with the solemn tone he's in the habit of using when he does.

Personally, the death penalty no longer concerns me at all. After what's happened, it wouldn't surprise me if I deserved it or underwent it. I'm the comrade of the soldier condemned to be shot. I'm the brother of the first man condemned to the death penalty. What matters to me is for men to avoid the crime of earning the death they deserve.

Mister Alba tells me:

"It's a grotesque anachronism to be thinking in these times of establishing the death penalty. The death penalty is dead all over the world. Between the man who laughs and the man who's in jail, they've put an end to it. To revive it would be to revitalize a ghost. Capital punishment underwent the fate of the duel on the field of honor. Both perished without honor on the historical field of universal ridicule."

THURSDAY, OCTOBER 29

What pleases me about free school is the simple fact
that it's called free.
  Roger Peyrefitte

We've got into the habit where Mister Alba gives a lecture
in the cell every Thursday. The days when Mister Alba
does his public speaking, as we might call it, David calls
our cultural Thursdays.

As is customary, today Mister Alba is filling his role with
full solemnity. Standing, he puts a dark-tinted monocle in
his eye, not the good one but the empty one. Then, as he
keeps taking off and putting on his hat, he starts to speak.
I take something like stenographic notes on what he says.

"Ladies and gentlemen: my topic for today concerns an
unappreciated genius of our national literature. It's almost
unnecessary for me to say that I'm referring to the master
Vargas Vila, the only genius and the only unappreciated
person in Colombian literature. I think that Vargas Vila
was a real mess as a novelist. The same can be said of his
interpretations of a religious character. But his literary criti-
cisms, his historical studies, some of his political ideas
deserve consideration. Vargas Vila isn't read very much
today, but just the same he is read. In times past everybody

read him; his enemies so they could learn the art of defamation; his friends in order to learn how to write badly. But the fact is that he wrote quite well and the evidence is that after his death his books keep on speaking for him. Vargas Vila was the *enfant terrible* of Latin America, actually the *vieux terrible* of the turn of the century. Today his philosophical anarchism surprises no one. We may not be far away from a partial rehabilitation of his work. His life, of course, can no longer be rehabilitated. Vargas Vila is dead."

Mister Alba takes a bundle of papers from the pocket of his coat and takes some handwritten notes from it. It's what he calls his confidential file. With these in his hand he continues speaking.

"A lecturer must speak with the proof in his hands. Here is the proof of what Vargas Vila is worth. Jorge Luis Borges, the most important Spanish American writer of our time (if a European writer of German culture and English sensibility born in Argentina can be Spanish-American), Borges, I repeat, has said that all of Vargas Vila's work could be done without, but that one single sentence of his on the gallows belongs to immortality. Although Borges would seem to be right, there are many pages of Vargas Vila that belong to immortality. Few times has a writer ever been so concise in defining a man or calling attention to a situation. Permit me to show why."

Mister Alba takes out his monocle as though he wished to see better with his damaged eye and, consulting his notes, he continues speaking:

"Ladies and gentlemen, take your hats off to the high paint of insult. On Latin poetry, Vargas Vila says that Ovid was a brothel canary. On Panama, the apostle states that Colombia wasn't mutilated by iron but by gold. The master calls Yankees the traveling salesmen of venality. Of a politician who died, the avenger takes his leave in this way:

peace be with his belly. On love Vargas Vila says that women have something good that they hide but that when they don't hide it, it ceases to be good. On human activities the giant says that from the highest step of the gallows his enemies will always be beneath him. And, he adds, *'I have a pedestal of enemies.'* On the Mexican monarchy the republican says that Iturbide, because his head was empty, decided to put a crown on it. On himself the loner recognizes that his work is a road sown with ruins. On freedom the rebel maintains that suffering tyranny is the basest form of deserving it. I hope these quotes are sufficient to show you that this corrosive Colombian libelist was not the man of the single sentence that Borges speaks of."

Mister Alba takes a breath and continues: "Ladies and gentlemen: I've mentioned freedom. Freedom was Vargas Vila's great passion. He loved it so much that he kept it chained to his feet as though it were a domestic animal of his exclusive ownership. In conclusion, Vargas Vila is an ideal writer for prisoners. I don't know why Antón Castán doesn't take up reading him. Every book of the master's is a spade with which this gravedigger of myths fertilizes the singed tree of freedom day by day. Freedom excited him, revealed him, inflamed him. Vargas Vila was a nympho-maniac of freedom."

Mister Alba doesn't wait for any applause.

Braulio, as always dedicated to polishing the shoes with which he's going to leave jail, ventures to ask:

"Would you explain to me, Mister Alba, why you speak to us saying ladies and gentlemen?"

"Only a house painter would think of asking that. 'Ladies and gentlemen': that's how orators who respect ladies always start."

FRIDAY, OCTOBER 30

The institution of executioner is of divine origin.
　Joseph de Maistre

The idea of the death penalty hasn't left us any peace over the past few days. It's like a fly buzzing restlessly over our heads. It alights here and there, releases its larvae of anxiety in our minds and flits off to another spot as it goes about ceaselessly fertilizing what it has itself gestated.

We've just had our evening meal. David drops onto his bed and starts talking.

"I've read there's a jail in China where free men fight over having their turn in the honor of filling the role of executioner. By murdering, legally, men get rid of that relentless tendency toward murder, which seems to be a basic necessity for human beings. Thanks to these temporary executioners in China they've succeeded in getting a notable decrease in crime statistics."

Mister Alba adds a note:

"Henry Allen, the executioner in London, said that confinement is worse than the gallows. Still, sometimes I think it's too bad capital punishment doesn't exist in our country. There are a lot of people who deserve it."

70

"If capital punishment existed in our country," David goes on to say, "I'd like to try something a little more novel than what they practice in that jail in China. I'd like to make use of a democratic system where every condemned man could choose his own death. That is, each one would choose, in accordance with his own likes, the form of his particular execution."

"What about you, David, what execution would you choose?" Braulio asks.

"I hadn't thought about it."

"Well, think about it. What execution would you choose?"

"If I were condemned and could choose the form of my death, I'd choose the maximum penalty in English culture, namely hanging. It's a rough death but it has its compensations. Before the English adopted it, in their usual custom of taking over everything that belongs to the rest of the world, the noose was considered a dishonor. The English nationalized the noose and gave it distinction. Since there are fewer and fewer executions, people today are starting to look upon it as a civilized practice. After all, hanging isn't any more degrading than other forms of legal murder. Besides, hanging is like a woman, it takes away strength but it gives pleasure."

David's about to say something else when Braulio's voice is heard once more.

"You, Mister Alba, what kind of death do you prefer?"

Mister Alba has no other recourse but to think about what type of death he would choose. He understands that it's not a matter of death, really, but of talk. Of talk and filling that deep next-to-the-last void of the day with words.

"I'd prefer the electric chair," Mister Alba says. "I live under the influence of American civilization. I'd like for them to seat me on the electric chair, provided that before they throw the switch they allow me to calm my thirst with some ice-cold Coca-Cola. The electric chair is a technical way of killing at least. With it the barbarism of classical tortures disappears: It doesn't crack your bones like the vile and edifying garrote of the Spaniards, and it isn't inflammable like German cultural procedures where they inject gasoline into the veins of Jewish children. The bonfire is a savage torture, fit for the purification of the rotten blood of Swiss witches. The lash is a sadistic torture, good for bringing on bloodletting in the demonized flesh of Russians possessed by evil spirits. The joint science of living and dying owes the United States two great discoveries: the shower bath and the electric chair. The shower is to hygiene what the electric chair is to penal science. That is, the most pleasant way to wash as the other is the simplest way to kill. I vote for the electric chair, or, in other words, I vote for the United States."

David interrupts him:

"You, Braulio, what death would you choose?"

He's obliged to take part in the macabre game that he himself has invented. He doesn't hesitate to answer:

"I'd like a firing squad because it's a death for men. It's not a death for sex hounds like the noose or a death for mechanics like the electric chair. But I'd really prefer the guillotine. One quick slice and it's all over. A slice that divides life into two deaths: the death of the separated head and the death of the independent body. There's no doubt but that the guillotine is a typical invention of French culture."

"Have you read any books about the guillotine?" David asks me.

"I only read books about prisoners," I reply. "I'm not a specialist in executions."

The bell rings suddenly and we all feel a shiver. Tonight, calling for silence, the bell seems to be tolling for death.

Mister Alba speaks to me anxiously, as if something is urging him to make me answer quickly:

"You, Antón, what kind of death would you prefer?"

I don't answer immediately. They're all waiting for my words, because in the approaching circle of night and the strict haste of the rules there's still room for a few words.

"What type of death would you prefer, Antón?"

I still don't answer. But they all know that I'm going to answer. For the second and last time the bell rings, calling for the silence that's beginning to be heard. I have time to say four words:

"I prefer being innocent."

SATURDAY, OCTOBER 31

Many unfortunates have been condemned for heresy
simply because they're weak in grammar.

Morris West

David, Mister Alba, and Braulio insist that I read them the
diary. I resist, telling them it's not proper for a writer to
read what he's writing to people around him, all the more
so if what's being written is still unfinished, with no revi-
sions or corrections.

"That doesn't matter," David insists. "We want to know
what it is you're writing."

"Read it, please, Antón," Braulio begs.

"If we're characters in the novel, we've got a right to
know how you've pictured us," Mister Alba says.

"In the first place," I claim, "it's not a novel, it's a diary.
I stated that quite clearly. In the second place, if anyone
has got any rights to this work, that person is me."

"In any case, whatever it is, just read it to us. I want to
see myself living in your book."

Mister Alba's voice is so insinuating as he speaks these
words that I've got no recourse except to do what they
want. That business of seeing Mister Alba living intrigues

me. The pages already make up a respectable bundle. I start reading. It goes on without any interruptions.

The three of them are hanging on my words. Not one single time do they stop me. Braulio's face has no expression, but David nods with every paragraph. There are times when he can't hold back a smile. At other times his face betrays a certain hidden bitterness. Mister Alba keeps taking off and putting on his hat, which means that with each movement he's tipping his hat in homage to the author.

I don't know how long the reading lasts. I'm tired. My eyes are burning. But I don't stop until I've read the last word in the previous chapter.

"It's quite good," David says.

"Wonderful!" Braulio shouts.

I know that Braulio here is the stimulus of the public, that his voice is the voice of the people. It gives me a certain pride.

"You like it?" I ask him.

"A lot," he says. "That part about the rat really got to me. But it's not true that I envy you because it sleeps in your shoes."

"Speaking of the rat," I say, "for the first time in a long while it didn't sleep here last night. I'd like to know what's happened to it. It would be a shame if it doesn't come back."

Braulio looks disturbed.

Mister Alba has taken a long time to prepare his opinion, and he finally speaks.

"It's a novel. Nothing but a novel."

"It's a diary," I insist.

"The form may be that of a diary, but underneath it all it's a novel," Mister Alba declares.

"It seems more like a play to me," David observes. "The cell, the lack of action, dialogue, the psychological setting: the whole thing's a play. Notes for a play, stories for a play."

"The thing you're describing is called a novel," Mister Alba says.

"What Antón has just read is the first act of a play," David reaffirms.

Braulio has no literary opinions but he's quite interested in the opinions of the others.

"The novel doesn't favor me too much," Mister Alba says.

"I've limited myself to copying down everything you've said. Your speech on Vargas Vila was taken down in shorthand."

"I'm not referring to my words, which as usual are unobjectionable," Mister Alba says. "I'm referring to my actions, I mean the work you've put into describing them. You paint me as a ridiculous old man who tells a lot of jokes."

"It's not my fault if you don't act any other way."

"From today on I'll have to measure my words."

"Do whatever you think is right. I'll keep on writing my diary."

"You can go on writing your novel," Mister Alba repeats, determined to put his critical opinion forward.

"I still insist it's a play," David emphasizes. "The first act is just about to end. If the choreographic element strays on occasion, sometimes toward a novel, sometimes toward an essay, other times toward a poem, and always with the format of a diary, it doesn't take away the work's theatrical character. My advice to you is when you finish, don't write 'The End,' but 'The Curtain Falls.'"

Encouraged by these ideas, I draw my own conclusions.

"Everything you people are saying and what I think after having read what's written up till now makes me remember that I've always considered we're on the threshold of a literature of synthesis. The classic literary genres as such tend to disappear because they're becoming fused.

I don't know whether it's a show of strength or a sign of weakness. In any case, nowadays you don't write just for the initiated or just for the illiterate. These days literature is being channeled down into a single stream of general culture that's got everything in it. I feel quite satisfied to hear you say that my book brings together novel and diary, play and poem without being any one of them because it's all those things at the same time."

"As far as poetry's concerned, I don't see any poetry in the row of prisoners in the book," David says.

"I'm the poem," says Mister Alba.

Mister Alba takes off his hat, puts the monocle in his useless eye, and bows to me.

"What's that all about, Mister Alba?" Braulio asks.

"I'm rehearsing my part. David is right. Let's start acting. For myself, from now on I'll have to rehearse every step I take. Glory's not going to catch me off guard."

SUNDAY, NOVEMBER 1

It was necessary to be there with those who were fighting for justice, not with those who denied justice.

Arturo Uslar Pietri

Mister Alba cleans his safety razor and says:

"All right. I'm ready. Let's begin."

"Begin what?" Braulio Coral asks.

"Begin today's rehearsal for Antón's play."

"It's not a play," I correct him. "I'm only writing down what happens."

"Antón is the jail's chronicler," David explains. "He's our war correspondent. The correspondent of our war with freedom," Braulio Coral finishes.

As can be seen from what he's just said, over the past few days Braulio has been making a notable improvement in his way of speaking from listening to us. When he gets to put on the shiny shoes he works on every day and goes free, it could be said that he will have received an education in jail and that imprisonment has been of great use to him.

"About this correspondent business," I comment, "I'd like to have a few declarations from you to put in my diary, Mister Alba."

David looks at me, offended.

"Speaking literally," he says. "We couldn't get any lower. We're touching bottom. We've reached journalism."

Mister Alba pays no attention to him and gets ready to answer. He looks like a statesman surrounded by a gang of ruffians at a press conference. Observing Mister Alba's preparatory adjustments, David comments:

"For absolute degradation all that's missing are the photographers."

"We'll talk about photography later," I say.

Mister Alba places himself placidly at my disposal, saying:

"I'm ready."

"Well, Mister Alba," I begin. "How many countries have you visited?"

"You should say what are the countries that have traveled inside me. But, speaking in the geographical and political terms of today, I know thirty-eight countries. In reality, the countries I've been to in a different period are only eleven. The other twenty-seven belonged at the time to the British Empire. With the dismemberment of the British Empire my collection of independent nations grew notably."

"What's your opinion of colonialism?"

"The only good thing about colonialism is that it paved the way for decolonization."

"Could you tell us something about your past?"

"I have no past. I only have a present. That is to say, I only have a future. Master Vargas Vila said that the present is the future that's passing."

"Why do you quote Vargas Vila so much?"

"If I didn't quote him who would?"

"Did you know Master Vargas Vila personally in your youth?"

"No. Luckily I never had to face that danger."

"Is Vargas Vila your favorite writer?"

"I don't fall in love with writers. I only have favorite books."

"Could you tell us something about your family, if it's not too much trouble?"

"It's no trouble because luckily I do have a family. My father's name was Sebastian Torra y Alba, which is my name too. My father..."

"Just a minute. Why do they call you Mister Alba?"

"Mister Alba is a nickname that's almost a name. Through the Alba I come from the grandees of Spain. Through the Mister from the peewees of Panama. It was in Panama that they baptized me Mister Alba."

"What's your opinion of feminism?"

"What the devil does feminism have to do with jail?" David asks indignantly.

"Journalistically speaking, the question is pertinent," Mister Alba says. "The duty of a good reporter is to formulate all manner of stupid questions. Well, in my day, back in 1930, feminism still hadn't been masculinized. Today you can't speak of feminism. The feminists of 1930 have grown moustaches. In those days I knew a rabid feminist who, when she quoted Homer, didn't say Trojan horse but Trojan mare."

"Do you have a word for your admirers?"

"The only ones who admire me are judges."

"What can you tell me regarding your religious beliefs?"

"In matters of religion I'm faithful to the faith of my elders. When I'm a prisoner I'm a full-time believer. When I'm free, I'm a Catholic only on Sundays."

"You speak with such eloquence that you remind me of the Senate. I was in the Senate four years ago," I tell Mister Alba.

"You were a senator?"

"No, I was a stenographer."

As proof of that stenographic experience I take careful notes of everything Mister Alba says. Watching me, he asks:

"Can I be sure that you're not deforming my thought?"

"Absolutely sure. I'm taking notes in shorthand."

"Can't shorthand make mistakes?"

"It makes mistakes but it's a lot more faithful than memory. And, speaking of proofs of faithfulness, do you have a photograph to illustrate the interview, Mister Alba?"

Mister Alba takes his confidential file from his pocket, unties the string that holds the package together, shuffles through the papers, and places a photo in my hands. He hands it to me and then Braulio and David pounce on the picture where a very good-looking man dressed in clothes of a bygone style is trying desperately to look like Mister Alba.

"You look very young in this picture," David says.

"I don't look young," Mister Alba says. "I look good, which is a different matter. The reason is quite simple. When I have my picture taken I pay five pesos for the photo and fifteen pesos for the touch-up."

"In line with all this, Mister Alba, could you say something about your age?"

"The only thing I can tell you about my age is that I haven't missed a single minute of this century. The twentieth century was born with me. That's why we understand each other."

"How would you define yourself for posterity?" I ask in conclusion.

Mister Alba replies without hesitation:

"I'm a prisoner. Nothing more, nothing less than a prisoner. I know my destiny. In other words, I'm a man. A man, that is to say, a tragic humorist."

The interview is over. Several guards are coming down the hallway. They reach the door and open it. One of them pushes in a cart full of clothing.

"How many people here?"

"Four," Braulio Coral answers.

"Four," the head man repeats in an imperative tone.

The man with the cart takes out eight prison suits, consisting of pants and a shirt. He gives four items to each of us. The cloth is of a thick material, more appropriate for quarry workers than prisoners.

"What's this?" David asks.

"The uniform," the head man answers. "From today on everybody in the jail will have to wear it."

Mister Alba examines the shirts. They carry a number on the chest. I draw 223. All of this makes Mister Alba indignant.

"Leloya is a fast worker," he says. "How much has Colonel Leloya made in the deal for these uniforms?"

No one answers, but after a pause the guard asks Mister Alba:

"What is it you don't like about the uniforms?"

"I don't like the jail's being mechanized. I'm an old prisoner, which is like saying I'm an old Christian, or an old sinner. I don't want the jail to lose its freedom."

Mister Alba has something more to say. Mister Alba doesn't want there to be any peace.

"I'm not putting on this crap," he states.

"We'll see about that," the head guard says. "In any case, I'll inform Colonel Leloya."

"You can tell your Colonel Leloya that he can go take a shit for himself," Mister Alba says.

"Don't you insult the colonel, because I'll put you in the stocks."

"I can see that your Colonel Leloya's reorganization's going to be thorough. Not only does he force us to wear this stinking uniform, which doesn't even have the professional charm of stripes, but he's already setting up the stocks, which haven't been used since the days of the Holy Inquisition. Hurray for prison reform!" Mister Alba shouts, taking off his hat.

The head guard makes use of the occasion to hit him on the head with his rifle butt. Mister Alba falls to the floor. The guards withdraw. One of them goes along pushing the cart full of prison reform down the corridor.

"Are you all right, Mister Alba?" Braulio asks as he wipes the blood from his forehead with some toilet paper.

"I'm fine," Mister Alba answers. "All in all, I've been taught a lesson. I'll never mention prison reform again. From here on in I'll only concern myself with freedom reform."

David says:

"Every kind of prison reform is like that. In France the guillotine was the result of a prison reform. Thanks to prison reform in Utah you can choose between the rope and a firing squad."

To drive away the sad consequences of the incident a little, I say:

"While the door was open I was able to get a good look at the hallway. It's full of prisoners. They look like peasants."

"They are peasants," Braulio explains. "My lawyer told me yesterday. They took over the estates where they were working and divided up the land. They all ended up in jail."

Mister Alba has the virtue of making a quick recovery. He says:

"Agrarian reform for rich people on estates consists of jailing the peasants who anticipate agrarian reform on their own with farms for the poor."

A short time later Mister Alba adds, in a confidential tone, addressing me:

"In your chronicle of the day don't even think about repeating that bit about Colonel Leloya's going to take a shit for himself. In jail and with Leloya it's fine. But in the disinfected protocol of freedom, no. You've got to respect your readers above all."

"Don't worry, Mister Alba," I answer. "I'll eliminate that passage. Since we're locked up and emptying buckets, I've learned how to keep the cell clean."

MONDAY, NOVEMBER 2

All evils are born in a state of innocence.

    Ernest Hemingway

At night before we go to sleep, a drop of light, who knows why, filters in through the window and dissolves in the blackness of the cell.

No one's asleep, but we can't talk anymore. Other glimmers of light come and go. The momentary gleams pass so rapidly that tonight David can't punish the light as he did the night when he spat on the moon.

I think about the moon and I know David's thinking about it, too. The moon demoralizes and irritates him. Among other things the moon also drives Nancy away.

Nancy comes to visit David every night. Nancy's the fifth occupant of the cell. He starts waiting for her early on, taken with fear and enchantment. Sometimes she'll come on the wings of a poor moth who mistakenly falls into the restless grasping of his arms. On clear nights David's rage derives from the fact that the moon chases Nancy's visits away.

Nancy makes me think of a woman I love and have never met. I know that this woman exists and that she was born for me. Sometimes the jail makes me think that I'll never get to know her, and that before I can find her we'll both die in a state of useless purity, even though we're perfect for each other. But I also keep on thinking that someday I'll find her. In the cell I can't go out to look for her, but at night in the broad world all the stars are seeking her for me.

The moon occupied a very peculiar place in my childhood dreams. In the cell, the presence of the moon or its evocation permits me to live in one night two distinct nights that are distant in space and time. I live them there at the same time, with a double life, with the innocent criterion of a child and the mature judgment of a convict.

Once when I was eleven my father took me to see the sea. With the small dribbles of light that come and go tonight I'm close to living a night by the sea again. The moon falls over the sea. It's not that the moon has come to bathe in the sea. It's that the moon has come to live with the sea. Still timid, before merging, they admire each other, approach, kiss. Finally they blend, like two crazed lovers. Now the sea changes into moon curd.

My father and I decide to have a swim in the moon. Submerged, we don't feel that we're in the water but in a lake of the moon. For a long time we splash about in that lake of light. When we come out we're still dripping moonlight. We're equally divided into man and sea and moon. In the sand we leave the salty footprints of the moon.

Another unforgettable feeling that's related to the moon is more recent. I'm in a country house high in the Andes a few days before I'm arrested. In the clear Andean light I see an artificial satellite cross the sky.

I know that it's a satellite because it moves like a star. I know that it's artificial because it has the humiliated regularity of something governed by the hand of man. Also, because in the vast firmament that ball of light doesn't run along the way stars do when they go mad.

That night makes me think on this night I'd like the job of astronaut.

Diogenes looked for a man. Columbus looked for a continent. The astronaut looks for a world. The universe has expanded a little since the mathematicians of twenty-five centuries ago dared suppose that the sun was larger than Greece.

Next to the sea on Santa Marta Bay we lived in a cabin that belonged to a friend of my father's. I can't recall anything about the long trip by river from the interior to the Caribbean coast. But I can't forget the moon and the bay. I also remember that the cabin was under the care of a black man from Jamaica. He's a mystical man and belongs to the sect of Seventh Day Adventists.

The black man owns a mangy, skinny cat who plays with me. According to the Jamaican the cat's an Adventist, too. He claims the cat won't eat meat on Saturdays. What really happens is that on Saturdays the Jamaican condemns the cat to complete hunger after having trained him in partial hunger during the whole week. That cat dedicated to religious abstinence moves me to pity.

That moves me to pity. For several days I go about trying to catch a live mouse, aiming to test on some Saturday how authentic is the moral strength of the cat's fast. But I never get to do it for lack of a mouse.

In the bed next to mine David is restless, caught up in pleasure and pain at the same time.

Raymond Cartier has said that in the drama of the universe there's nothing as pathetic as the suicide of whales when they come in huge bands to die on the land that belonged to them millions of years ago.

That item of Cartier's, which I read sometime back, leads me to think tonight about the man from Jamaica. I remember the black man sitting and facing the sea. He stays there for three hours, withdrawn, sadly contemplating the surface of the sea. On the water, however, there's nothing to be seen. No flying fish, no floating logs, no ships loaded with bananas. Only tonight as I listen to David near me have I come to discover why the Jamaican scrutinizes the sea with that unhealthy and touching insistence.

It's not a question of contemplation but of an ancestral call. The man from Jamaica is linked to the sea by the umbilical cord of nostalgia.

Along the intimate path of blood, through millenniums of memory, pilgrimage, and pain, the man from Jamaica keeps watch on the sea for his ancient homeland, in the sea he smells the maternal uterus, in the sea he seeks the remote miracle of God. In the sea he looks for the primitive cave of the species, just like the prodigal whales, just like the man who on his first night of freedom returns to sleep in the jail he has left.

I can also bring back another episode linked to our life in the cabin. On the bay, as along almost all the Caribbean coast, children up to the age of ten or twelve always go naked. But let's be specific: only the boys, not the girls. It can be seen that girls, from an early age, are subject to the immodesty of an uneven rivalry.

My father explains to me that the heat is the cause of male nudity. That idea doesn't seem acceptable to me today. It's obvious and the evidence is plentiful that heat is a euphemism to describe poverty. In any case, there's no indecent or professional elaboration in that nakedness of children. It's a case of automatic nudity here.

Balzac tells the moving story of two children contemplating a painting of the earthly paradise. One of them asks which is Adam. The other says that he can't tell because the two figures are naked.

In the paradise of Santa Marta you can tell, without blushing, which one is the male. The male is the one who's naked.

Near the cabin the tide tosses up a lot of wood on the beach, slavered with ancient fury by the tongue of the sea. In the remains of that vegetative flotsam my childish curiosity finds all manner of shapes. There are hands with five fingers and four fingernails, as though bringing to mind the work of a sharp carving knife; there are cats with whiskers and feet but no tail, as though the zoological, mutilated stick meant to inspire pity in us for the Jamaican's cat; there are the pretty faces of girls with an ear placed at the beginning slope of her mountain of hair, as if indicating that female monsters, just like Mister Alba's Tolabo Indians, also talk with their ears on their foreheads.

Only tonight have I discovered the truth. In that pile of sticks gnawed by the sea, nature isn't imitating art. What surfaces here is a phenomenon of that typically cubist cult of personality. The sea is imitating Picasso.

I've always wondered what could have brought Endymion and Caligula to fall in love with the moon. There's something I don't understand in that passion. Falling in love with the moon is crazy. I can't understand either why on moonlit nights Mister Alba hides from it. I asked him once and he told me:

"According to the interpretation of the article that defines it in many ancient and modern languages, the moon belongs to the male sex. It's best to be sure. To put it briefly, it might fall in love with me."

In the mythology of the jail, for David, at least, there's no place for loving the moon. David, on the other hand, is in love with darkness. Every night the unaccompanied darkness brings him the aroma of Nancy's body. Facing him the darkness loses all its modesty. Passion lies in wait for him with no echo of himself. Darkness is the path that opens up for David the gates of paradises predicted or forgotten. I can hear the poor devil in the darkness. I don't pity him because I know that in those moments at least he's not alone.

Sometimes David covers the barred window that looks out on the courtyard, sticking up a piece of cardboard on the inside. In that way David tries to stop the darkness from escaping out of his hands, to stop the darkness from slipping away through the courtyard window.

On the brink of sleep I recall the night when David spat at the moon. The moon had come out early. The bell hadn't rung yet. As usual, David was talking about Nancy with the voice of a man who is expecting a woman.

"We would go horseback riding through the trees to the river. While I got the fishing pole ready, Nancy unsaddled the horse and took off her clothes. She sat waiting for me on the horse. Have you ever been on a horse with a girl, Mister Alba?"

"I'm not a cowboy or an acrobat," Mister Alba answered. "When it comes to women, I'm a man from terra firma."

That allusion really bothered David. The shadows were already closing in, depositing the quiver of Nancy's youth in his blood. David spat with fury at the moonbeam.

The moonbeam fled through the window, frightened by the madness of that man who was looking for Nancy in the cell but finding only the sterile lips of darkness.

In any case, when David kisses it, the darkness starts to quiver.

TUESDAY, NOVEMBER 3

How can you save someone who doesn't want to be saved?

    Par Lagerkvist

Sometime after mid-afternoon several guards approach the cell. They open the door and shove in a man who almost falls into the midst of us.

"Starting today this will be your nest, Fatso," a guard says.

"What's this business about this being his nest?" Mister Alba asks.

"Those are my orders," the guard states.

"There are four of us here and four's already too many for the cell," Braulio Coral exclaims. "With one more we'll all suffocate."

"If they're sending in another one, it's most likely that one of you is going to leave. In any case, there's nothing I can do about it. Fatso stays here."

The guards shut the door and leave and the stranger is left with us.

"Allow me to introduce myself," he says. "My name is Antonio Tudela. In the squad they called me the Honorable Fatso Tudela."

"What squad's that?" I ask.

"The detective squad. The secret police. I worked in the foreign section."

"Are you a spy, then?" Mister Alba asks.

"Spy, no. Detective. That's all. I was successful chasing men but I failed at chasing news. Before I was a detective I worked on a newspaper as a police reporter."

Mister Alba comments:

"From police reporter to detective and from detective to criminal. Not a bad background for success in jail."

"Where are you from?" David asks.

"From Sonsón. I'm one of the Tudelas of Sonsón."

He says "one of the Tudelas of Sonsón" with a stressed humility for family and place, with a simplicity that takes precedence over any historical complications, as though he'd said he was one of the Bonapartes of Corsica.

"What happened for you to end up here?"

"A foreigner. An Arab peddler. When I was arresting him my gun went off and killed him. It's an outrage for them to put me in jail."

He tells it in such a natural way that he's quite convincing in that his crime was an accident.

Braulio takes the floor:

"In return for your friendly attention, let me introduce you to your cellmates. You're in luck. It so happens that you share this cave with men who live only for matters of the spirit. As Mister Alba says, jail is the only refuge left for philosophy because it's the only ivory tower remaining in the world. There are social classes in jail, too, the same as outside. Near here there's a prisoner, a fellow named Toscano, a black marketer in necessities, who's got a deluxe apartment with a double bed, television, refrigerator, and a private secretary. We're not so opulent in material possessions. This is a cell of intellectuals. Here they are before you."

He stops speaking, looks at David, points to him, and continues:

"This is David Fresno, writer. He wrote his uncle's name on some bad checks."

The Honorable Fatso Tudela doesn't know whether Braulio is kidding or telling the truth. It's a rather strange introduction. He hesitates between not doing anything and offering David his hand. Braulio goes on talking.

"This is Antonio Castán. Keep your eye on him because he's the chronicler of the jail. Antón is a professional innocent."

As he looks at me the Honorable Fatso Tudela is still hesitant. Braulio points to Mister Alba.

"Here you have the great Mister Alba. For a man like you, involved in foreign matters, I guess his name tells you everything."

"It doesn't tell me a thing."

"If jail didn't exist the police would have to invent it so they could give Mister Alba's image its proper frame."

"Why is he a prisoner?" the Honorable Fatso Tudela asks.

"For being an internationalist. Mister Alba is a specialist in Confidential International Law."

"I don't see any reason for arresting him for that."

"It's a long story. He set up his own a consulate of the United Nations in Quito and set about selling fake passports of every nationality. A lot of jails claimed the honor of having Mister Alba behind their bars. He was extradited because of other previous moments of weakness and the Ecuadorean authorities sent him here. Mister Alba is a patriot. He only likes the jails in Colombia."

David interrupts him:

"Let me relieve you, Braulio. Señor Tudela, this is Braulio Coral. He's in jail because of a mistake. His only crime is loving too much."

"Love?" the Honorable Fatso Tudela asks.

"He fell in love with two women at the same time."

"Falling in love isn't a crime, it would seem to me."

"But getting married is," Mister Alba says with no further explanation.

I get the impression that the Honorable Fatso Tudela is puzzled. He obviously understands foreign affairs but not bigamy.

Mister Alba takes off the medal on his lapel and starts polishing it.

"Why are you cleaning your medal?" Braulio asks.

"Today is the national holiday of Panama. It doesn't mean anything to you people, but for me, who'll soon be old and who's lived there, well, I want to celebrate it."

"You celebrate the independence of Panama by polishing a medal from Colombia?"

Mister Alba pays no attention to David's impertinent question. He limits himself to a patriotic reflection:

"National integrity is quite important, but sometimes mutilation is salvation. Today Colombia and Panama are what they ought to be. Master Vargas Vila reduces the Panama question to a bullfight. He said that when Panama was sliced off, Colombia simply had its tail cut off."

A preoccupation has been troubling my mind for a while now. I finally can't hold it back:

"The guard said that if they sent in somebody new it's because someone else is going to leave. I wonder who it is?"

"I know."

And as if there's no doubt about it, Braulio Coral picks up his shoes, the ones that will lead him to freedom, and he starts shining them over the shine they already have.

The Honorable Fatso Tudela is one of those men who makes a good impression from the first moment he's locked up in jail. The Honorable Fatso Tudela is squatting in a corner and I tell him:

"If you're tired, take my bed."

But he doesn't answer. He stays there crouching, huddled in the darkest corner of the cell.

"He's suffering from detective's nostalgia," Mister Alba says. "He's thinking back to when he used to crouch in the dark ready to shoot at innocent people."

A short time later the rat appears. We all watch the spectacle in silence. Out of the corner of the cell full of books and newspapers where Fatso Tudela is crouching, a legion of ants emerges. The ones in front advance, retreat, and then advance again, as if they were testing the limits of the path which the ones in the rear are following confidently, but which the first go on probing indecisively. The ones in the middle are carrying a corpse. It's a funeral procession. The backs of the ants look like those of humans laden with the weight of death.

What the ants are carrying is a kind of pouch, which is all that's left of the rat. Worms can still be seen inside the empty stomach. I don't know why, but I get the feeling the worms are looking at me as if in the cell I was in there was nothing but a handful of a man's dust mixed in with a handful of coffin dust.

It must have been dead ever since it disappeared from our presence. If it died of poison, the poison must taste quite good to the worms and the ants. From that time on the worms sprouted out of the bosom of death and have had no rest until they've devoured all that was left of that life. Now the ants are carrying off the last spoils, the half-dried worm-eaten skin, to some safe refuge. In that residue of animal life the ants have found reserve rations for days of scarcity.

In a rage, Mister Alba throws the chain he'd bought to domesticate the rat onto the ants. The funeral caravan scatters. The ants run about madly. The chain smashes the skin whose remains fly all about the cell in the form of thin scales.

I remember something Mister Alba told me one day:

"If the death of a bird is a crime against life, the life of a rat is a crime against death."

With this spectacle I've just witnessed, for the first time I see myself overcome by the very breath of the jail. Until today the intellectual activity in the cell hadn't let me notice the prison acids that are penetrating me and corroding my bones. Boxed up in those ideas, until today I've been neglecting the other inmates, who are a prolongation of myself. To put it another way, I'm betraying myself in my fellows. The ivory tower of a cell exhibits me naked before the ones around me but it won't let me see them. I owe these discoveries to the rat. The rat has had the virtue of arousing and pushing toward me the dreary sense of the misery of that penal den.

I sense the reality of great human putrefaction prowling around my cell. An uproar of beasts is marauding about me and it brings on panic. I can smell and hear hunger, malnutrition, syphilis, tuberculosis, homosexuality, idleness, despair, ignorance, crime, superstition, villainy. All the decompositions of the body and soul piled by the door to my cell overwhelm and humble me.

In order to get rid of this stench of the living tonight, I shall have to whistle for the dead.

II
The Club

FRIDAY, NOVEMBER 6

I only obey violence.
  Arthur Koestler

8. A.M. Three days ago the slow motion in the cell changed into the vertigo of the courtyard. Events are taking on a rhythm that almost prevents me from writing. The diary is changing into an hour by hour accounting. At this rate I'll have to record every second of our lives. Right now I'm taking hurried notes in shorthand. I'll develop them later when the jail regains its calm.

11 A.M. Three days ago Braulio got his freedom back. It was a sad day for all of us.

In jail comedy goes along dogging the heels of tragedy. Braulio was so overcome with emotion at the moment of leaving that he forgot his shoes at the last minute. He'd spent a year getting them ready to lead him into freedom. The day he got it he lost his way and instead of wearing the gleaming shoes he left in the filthy rope sandals. When we noticed Braulio's oversight the Honorable Fatso Tudela looked at the shoes and said:

"Beautiful shoes. But without Braulio here they look like a pair of orphans who've lost their feet."

And he began to try on the freedom shoes.

In the course of twenty-four hours, the Honorable Fatso Tudela was already moving about the cell with exemplary and natural ease. He gave off the feeling that he'd spent his whole life with us.

Today Fatso is part of our secret life. Mister Alba tells me:

"For your information, it was Braulio who killed the rat. He killed it with his shoes the last time you were out with your lawyer."

2 P.M. The situation we find ourselves in began the night following the day when Braulio left the jail.

We weren't unaware that tempers were heating up in the jail and as though we had a foreboding of something, none of us could get any sleep. I thought that what was preventing us from getting to sleep was the empty space that Braulio's absence had left in us.

But there were other things that allowed one to presume a crisis was approaching. Colonel Leloya's appointment as warden was no small matter for those who were nourished on the fear of official acts of repression. The unjust detention of hundreds of peasants weary of the demagoguery about the promise of land who had decided to occupy it and divide it up themselves was a dangerously combustible material in the atmosphere of the jail.

Finally, there was another no less explosive ingredient. It was Leloya's decision to impose on the prisoners the penal uniform as well as other measures that restricted our already quite restricted freedom. Until just a few days before, our beloved jail had been a civilian prison where men dressed as they pleased and, in a certain way, in their personal appearance at least, did what they felt like doing. With that they had preserved their last illusion of free men.

When Leloya imposed the uniform, inspired by the universal jailer's concept that prisoners should not only be prisoners but should display on their bodies the stigma of their infamy, it wasn't just they felt the last vestige of freedom they had left was being taken away, but they came to the conclusion that this was the beginning of submission to a regime of force whose rigor in Leloya's hand had been familiar to many before.

Along toward midnight we became aware that something was going on. Groups of barefoot men were running stealthily along the hallways. A short time later shouts and shooting could be heard. Then men who were no longer barefoot ran through the hallways again. Somebody began opening the door of our cell. He was doing it with a key, but the chore was taking a long time, indicating that whoever was trying to get it open wasn't used to it.

Just as the door of our cell opened, the prison bell sounded the alarm. A man appeared in the cell door. He was a convict from a nearby cell whom we knew quite well. His name was Antonio Toscano.

"The peasants have revolted," Toscano announced. "There's a mutiny all through the jail. We're inviting you people to come out and join the fight."

We were all outside in a minute. We had trouble moving after the depressive immobility that had been forced on us for several weeks. At the end of the hallway three guards had had their weapons and uniforms taken away. They were prisoners and they were ridiculous prisoners, unarmed and in their undershorts.

In the main courtyard the prisoners had made a bonfire and were burning the prison files and the uniforms in it. Some people were acting crazy and dancing around the fire like Indians in a ritual dance. The bonfire where the tools of prison reform were burning symbolized freedom for them.

Mister Alba went back to the cell, got dressed up as a gentleman, with his felt hat and his monocle, and a moment later we had him by the bonfire. He threw his uniform into the flames. Then he shook his hands over the fire as if trying to purify in that way those hands soiled by carrying the mold of the inmates' humiliation.

Nobody thought for a moment about taking advantage of the riot to escape. It wasn't a criminal riot but a riot in the name of justice. Besides, nobody would have been able to do so. The four guards in the hallway were the only ones who'd fallen into the hands of the rioting peasants. The rest had managed to get away to a safe place with their weapons. After the first moment of confusion they'd regrouped their forces for retaliation. In addition, a moment later we heard the familiar sounds of freedom coming from the street around the jail. The sirens on police cars began to howl. Along the concrete pavement came the metallic moving chain sound of the tread of army tanks.

5 P.M. Making a unique noise with his wooden leg, Oscar arrives, accompanied by Toscano. Oscar is a friend of Mister Alba.

"The prisoners want us to set up a kind of steering committee and for you to head it," Oscar says, speaking to Mister Alba.

"A steering committee for what?" David asks.

"To manage the uprising," Oscar explains.

"What's to be done?" Mister Alba asks.

"I already told you. Manage the uprising. Organize the rebels. Ration supplies now and ration hunger later when supplies run out. Negotiate with Leloya, if it's necessary to negotiate with him. Run the war like a general. That's what has to be done."

From where I am I can see Oscar resting on his wooden leg. Oscar has the look of a bird of ill omen. He looks like a bird of prey roosting by one leg on a solitary rock.

At the same time the lack of a leg gives a certain distinction to his personality. Being rather timid as a child, I felt a secret envy of men who were missing a leg because the lack of it attracted attention. Combining my childhood beliefs and my experiences of today I know that men with just one leg are only found among heroes and convicts.

Mister Alba speaks immediately:

"Tell them I accept as long as I can organize the steering committee."

Oscar is doubtful for a moment.

"Who do you think should make up the committee according to the way you see it?"

"Those of us here," Mister Alba answers. "Antón, David, Fatso Tudela, Toscano, you, and me."

Oscar shows enthusiasm. That was evidently just what he'd been hoping for. Still, he has objections:

"Aren't we going to give any representation on the committee to the peasants? After all, they were the ones who started the uprising."

"They were the ones who started it, but we were the ones who won it," David says. "Revolutions are not for revolutionaries. The peasants are accustomed to voting without having representation."

Mister Alba decides:

"That's right. Besides, the peasants aren't needed now. It's not a question of agrarian reform but of war, like you said."

"All right," Oscar accepts. "I'm sure everybody will agree to your conditions."

He leaves, feeling now as a member of the committee, dragging his wooden leg along the flagstones of the courtyard. From the rear he looks like a beggar. His long beard is so thick that it can be seen from behind as it overflows his shoulders and chest in a great flow.

"Oscar?" I ask.

"A renegade priest," David informs me.

"I don't like renegade priests," Mister Alba says. "They hide their dagger with the same hand with which they display Christ."

"If you don't trust him, why'd you go along with him in this steering committee business?" I ask. "Why do you put him on it?"

"War and politics oblige us to do a lot of base things," Mister Alba says philosophically.

9 P.M. I'm already getting fatigued from taking notes. Events are moving faster than my shorthand.

The committee has just been set up. Mister Alba has been elected president and Oscar vice-president. David says a directorship made up of a one-eyed man and a cripple means good luck for our actions.

Toscano proposes that we have them take an oath.

"That's not necessary," the Honorable Fatso Tudela says. "And, besides, it would be useless. They're both experts in swearing falsely."

That makes us all laugh. The one who laughs the most is Oscar. Since his mouth can't be seen with the cascading hair of his beard, Oscar gives the impression that he's laughing with his beard. Every hair in it is a telegraph wire made to his insolent laugh into the air.

Toscano, who evidently is a jailhouse lawyer, then suggests that we appoint a recording secretary.

"We're not organizing a labor union," David says.

"If we set up a committee we've got to organize it according to the law. The law. The law above all," Toscano demands.

"The law is for free men," I say.

We get involved in a long argument about whether or not the law prevails in jail, too. Mister Alba and I say it doesn't. But nobody can get it into Toscano's head that the jurisdiction of the civil law doesn't cross the threshold of a jail. He thinks that we'll have to give an accounting of our actions later on, as if the committee were some kind of philanthropic society, and he thinks that our duty is to look after our health.

104

"This is a riot, not a contract," I say.

But Toscano insists on following the law. No one knows which law. Toscano talks about it with the emphasis of someone who cites the law in order to break it.

Mister Alba finally finds the proper solution. In a few words he defines the situation.

"All right. Antón Castán will continue being our recording secretary."

They're all satisfied, but Toscano then proposes that instead of calling the committee a committee we give the body the name of *junta*. Mister Alba can't take any more.

"Look here, Toscano," he says. "If what you want to do is sabotage the uprising, say so right out. I'm president and I run the committee. If you don't like belonging to it, I can dismiss you in two seconds."

Toscano doesn't say a word. But it's obvious that a rivalry has sprung up between the two men.

12 A.M. Shortly before midnight we ended the first session of the steering committee. Mister Alba has shown himself to be a formidable organizer.

He created a health group, entrusted with supervising the wash basins and collecting water. According to him there's no doubt that it won't take Leloya long to cut off the water. He established another group for food rationing, which is the one that has the biggest job. The kitchen and supply room fell into the rebels' hands at the first moment, so for a time we'll have more or less regular provisions.

But Mister Alba's main job has to do with what he himself calls our system of defense. Men chosen from among all the convicts will take turns preparing weapons with which to fight, gathering all the stones they can find, and stringing barbed wire with the wood from broken furniture. They will also keep watch on the movements of the government forces surrounding us. Organized too is a battalion charged with facing up to the bullets in case the guards try to move against us.

Everyone signs up for the suicide battalion. Daring is the one thing these men don't lack.

SATURDAY, NOVEMBER 7

Hour after hour Stroud would watch them slowly building
the machine destined to take his life.

    Thomas E. Gaddis

9 A.M. Above the prison offices is a terrace from which
you can observe the jail and everything around it.

In normal times there's always a platoon of guards armed
with assault rifles and carrying binoculars on the terrace.
This section of the jail was taken over and has been held
by the prisoners since yesterday. The armed guards disappeared during the course of the previous night, but when
they fled they left their binoculars behind.

I use a pair of binoculars to see what's going on in the
prison.

The jail is a building that dates back to colonial times.
The Spaniards didn't leave any memorable religious or
imperial architectural monuments in Colombia but they
did leave jails that were destined for immortality. The prison
building is massively heavy. It has the oppressive solidity
that a jail is supposed to have.

I've been told that this building was originally a
monastery. The cells of today's delinquents must have been
the cells of yesterday's penitents. I don't believe it. This

building was born a jail. Stones don't lie. If it was originally a monastery it must have been by means of some provisional adaptation or an occasional concession that can't be explained today.

The city surrounds the jail as though it were nourished by it and at the same time feared it. The city has imprisoned the prison. The houses surrounding it look like an unwanted prolongation of the jail. Seen from here the prison seems to be the heart of the small city. The jail no doubt represents and defines it more precisely than the site of the public school, more exactly than the façade of the church, more eloquently than the regional legislature building.

In other times our jail was called a *panopticon*, in others a penitentiary. They also had the gall to refer to it as a reformatory or correctional facility. Historians and poets called it an *ergastulum* and police reporters the hoosegow. At least today there aren't any leftovers of those pestilential words. The only prison reform that has brought about any evolution in the jail has been of a literary character, then, and it's a question of what to call it. The word jail fully expresses today what this place should be called.

On the tall towers that rise up at both ends of the jail, groups of armed guards watch us continuously, the same as we keep watch on all their movements. In this mutual binocular espionage there's an interchange of funereal flirtation. The towers are not modern enlargements of the building. They were born with it and they form an original part of its cold stone body. On each one, a bit ironically, two iron crosses rise up: these crosses were the origin of the legend that the jail had been a monastery.

I pick up the binoculars and observe the towers. With morning mist you can't see the crosses. But what you can see quite clearly is the new steel of the guards' rifles with telescopic sights aimed at the terrace with the millimetric precision of death.

3 P.M. At this time it looks for a moment that we are going to die.

The rifles sweep the terrace with their broom of lead. The prey they're after is evidently the steering committee that's operating from the terrace.

Mister Alba says:

"Let's be careful. Since we're going to die, let's show some fear."

But nothing happens. On the street the convicts can't fight without risk. On their own terrain they're a difficult target. We don't know whether or not the bursts are just a warning. I think they're due to the fact that up there on the the towers the armed guards share a little in the unarmed fear of the prisoners.

4 P.M. With the commotion of the past hour behind us now, from the back of the parapet I can observe the streets around the jail at my leisure.

Groups of civilians are gathering on the corners. They're probably interested in us. They're discussing what's to become of us. They're concerned, with evident enthusiasm, as to how the riot is progressing.

Outside other men parade by in front of the groups without joining them. These indifferent people walk as in a fog, somewhat the way the prisoners walk here inside. What pains me is that they're walking along the street without enjoying their freedom, almost as if they didn't realize they were free.

Behind the parapet I relate all this to David. He takes the binoculars and watches the automaton men parading up and down the streets of freedom. Holding onto the glasses, David says:

"If I could walk the streets the way they are, I'd go crazy from feeling myself free and start whooping."

Toscano informs us that Leloya has already ordered the water cut off. Thanks to the technical genius of Mister Alba,

who ordered abundant reserves stored up, we won't run
the risk of dying of thirst for several days.

5 P.M. On the terrace where we're huddled behind the
parapet Mister Alba tells me:

"Leloya wants to negotiate."

"It seems odd to me that Leloya's looking for a diplo-
matic way to put an end to this," I say.

"Leloya's attitude makes me suspicious, too. It's obvious they must be directing and controlling him from the
capital. If Leloya had the autonomy he had in other times
we would have been machine-gunned by now."

When he's alone with me Mister Alba acts and talks with
a simplicity I find confusing. It comes from the fact that
ever since I started writing this diary, without anyone's
knowing why, Mister Alba has begun to observe me like
an actor being paid to play an unforgettable role. He knows
it, too, and in public he acts exclusively for me. But Mister
Alba is always Mister Alba. Men are only sincere when
they try to deceive themselves. Mister Alba never seems
to me so sincere as when he starts to play the role of himself in life in my diary.

6 P.M. Along the street come nine black trucks that look
like freight cars. They're loaded to the brim with sacks of
barley. Around the platforms where they carry their cargo,
the trucks have metal bars that give them the look of
mobile cells. Men use bars as though they can't live without them.

Two blocks from the jail is a brewery, which is where
the barley is headed. At the brewery door something strange
takes place. Several men begin to unload the truck. But
the sacks of barley aren't turned over to the men from the
brewery waiting for them. They first pass through the hands
of a third group of men between those on the truck and

those from the brewery. According to Toscano those inter-mediaries have the job of collecting for a chain of black-marketers, a kind of trade union tax that in just half a minute raises the price of each bundle of barley by three pesos. Toscano adds that since it's after six o'clock the three groups of men can also collect their wages at overtime rates.

Toscano explains the process to me:

"From the municipal warehouses on through the load-ers, the drivers, the unloaders, the black-marketers, the price of the barley goes up by sixty percent. After the payment of government taxes, mortgage, agrarian loans, payments to the local political boss, the private loan shark, other token payments, the peasants who grow it working from sunup to sundown get only sixteen percent of the total value of the barley. Just enough for them to die of starvation, but under the rule of law and the grace of God."

"But why does the brewery put up with that?" I ask.

"The brewery can't do a thing. If it tries to do something for the peasants, it will be shut down by a strike of its workers. And as for the peasants, the sixteen percent is better than a work stoppage at the plant."

"There's nothing more fraternal than proletarian rivalry," Mr. Alba concludes.

"You're pretty well informed about the process of national beer production," I tell Toscano.

"It's only natural he should be," the Honorable Fatso Tudela explains. "Toscano's in jail for selling barley on the black market."

Toscano makes me think how a universal particular of injustice is the fact that all men can recognize it even when they all take part in it.

Down below in the prison courtyard the peasants seem discouraged with the slow course of the revolt.

They're in a hurry to get back to their fields and culti-vate the barley with the sweat of their brow so it can fatten the big vats in the brewery where the beer is aged.

On the terrace the slightly acrid, slightly sweet smell of the aging beer reaches right up to the nostrils of the mem-bers of the committee. Down below in the main courtyard the peasants are like mummies, numb with the Andean cold, wrapped in blankets, squatting under the black umbrellas of their huge hats. In the courtyard, cut off from the fresh air by the ancient walls, the peasants can't even enjoy the somewhat alcoholic, somewhat bitter smell of aging beer.

SUNDAY, NOVEMBER 8

How can you ask one of these people to take on the sins of them all?
    Carlos Fuentes

10 P.M. The prisoners are sleeping now. From every corner of the courtyard comes the hoarse and helpless sound of the peasants' sleep. At the spots designated for nighttime vigilance the volunteers stay awake.

We members of the committee gather on the terrace. Some one has put together a small pile of charcoal. In just a short while we have a little fire for light and heat.

There are still six of us on the committee. The four from the cell, Oscar, and Toscano. But tonight there's another one with us, someone spontaneous whose name I haven't been able to make out.

Toscano is the group's provisioner. He has the duty of making sure, it's not known by what means, that the committee is supplied with food. The steering committee has to eat and drink well because that's what the interests of the prisoners demand. When he reaches the terrace Toscano lays out on the ground a sack in which he has cigarettes, cheese, salami, hard-boiled eggs, cans of sardines, and a bottle of liquor.

Since we have no glasses because Mister Alba has ordered that all glasses be broken and the glass turned into sharp weapons, Toscano starts cracking the eggs. With a small stick he removes the insides, which he places-on a piece of paper. Then he begins serving the cane liquor in the eggshells.

I get a shellful of liquor and savor it. It tastes very good. It's food and drink at the same time. Taken in the eggshell the liquor has the flavor of both chicken and fermented and distilled cane juice. Toscano asks Mister Alba:

"What will you have to drink?"

"Piss on the rocks," Mister Alba replies.

"What did you say?" Toscano asks.

"He says he wants piss with ice," David translates.

Toscano has no reaction.

"I can serve you the piss," he says, "but the ice in the refrigerator's all gone."

The president of the steering committee doesn't find this answer amusing. It's one of those offenses that Mister Alba won't forgive.

"Don't you like cane liquor, Mister Alba?" I ask.

"A gentleman drinks only whiskey from Scotland," he says.

Toscano goes on serving the others. With the exception of Mister Alba, we're all eating bread and cheese.

With the third round of liquor Toscano takes a small guitar out of his bottomless sack and strumming it starts to sing. First he sings a Mexican song. It's rather fitting because it's a kind of jailhouse anthem, about shootings and police, a courtroom and a stone bed. Then he sings a Spanish song. The music is warm and melancholy. The lines go on about a green road that leads to a hermitage where a man remembers a woman.

Out of the bag Toscano takes two pieces of wood covered with slits. The notches are cut in order and are

114

visible, giving the impression that the wooden sticks are growing teeth.

Teeth isn't too far-fetched an image because a short time later the gums on the stick will start talking. It won't be real talking, however, because the voice will be a mixture of a whistle and a song.

"It's a *guacharaca*," Toscano explains. "Does anyone know how to play it?"

The Honorable Fatso Tudela says he knows how. He takes the sticks and starts rubbing them together with the look of a caveman working at making fire. At first it has a pained voice, everything reduced to a vegetable wail. Then little by little the rubbing of the sticks takes on rhythm and a primitive but soothing tone.

The music heats up and its echo spreads. Then something magical takes place. The light of the fire has gone out. The Honorable Fatso Tudela has disappeared. All you can see in the shadows are the two sticks his hands are rubbing together with diabolic fury. What's coming from his hands is a music that mingles with the origins of fire. Before being music it must have been a sacred rite, an explosion of elemental warmth. Suddenly, along with the music, sparks begin to pop out of the sticks. In a moment, in the invisible hands the music has changed into fire.

As they burn, the Honorable Fatso Tudela tosses the sticks away and one of them revives the coals of the fire for a moment. It has been a complete success. What no one knows is whether the musical action of the *guacharaca* always ends in flames or whether Fatso Tudela's enthusiasm became so great that he couldn't avoid the natural accident.

One of those present asks the president to close the session with a speech worthy of the circumstances. A born orator, Mister Alba doesn't need to have the request repeated.

"Ladies and gentlemen, you mustn't get the idea I'm going to recite any poetry. I'm not so low as all that. It's true that there might be some dumbbell in the audience"— Mister Alba stresses the word, looking at Toscano—"one of those dumbbells whose mentality can only be reached by a declaimer of poetry. But no, no. My motto is the following: I'd rather die than declaim. Jail would be a different place if the men here didn't declaim so much. Poetry deserves my respect. I take my hat off to it. But I don't take it off to reciters because reciters are traitors to lyric poetry, they're the ventriloquists of poetry."

Mister Alba takes off his hat, puts it back on, and continues speaking.

"Ladies and gentleman, I'm going to talk to you tonight about a performing artist I met in Mexico City, D. F. In the great nation of Mexico, Mexico is a walled city and its walls are called D. F., which stands for Distrito Federal. Well, there I got to know Cantinflas, the Charlie Chaplin of humoristic underdevelopment. Cantinflas is one of the greatest Latin Americans of all times. No fame is more deserved, because, a strange thing in Latin America, Cantinflas didn't win it by killing and oppressing but by making people laugh. Cantinflas is the comedian who has given humanity back to the poor Latin American man who's been maddened by a Samson complex. In this continent so full of villains, bosses, machos, leaders, masters, heroes, jailers, Cantinflas, standing naked before the laughter, has blown a little honor into authentic masculinity."

Mister Alba makes a motion with one foot. Something breaks under his shoe with the sound of a soft grain of rice. Mister Alba has squashed a cockroach. He immediately goes right on:

"Ladies and gentlemen, my great friend Leonidas Paeces, a Marxist poet, more Marxist than poet, once wrote, nevertheless, an unforgettable line. It went like this and don't think that I'm going to do any reciting for you: 'Chaplin, Chaplin, brother in shoes!' All right. Imitating him who, like Charlot, was born in broken down shoes, I can say like the great Paeces that Cantinflas is my brother in pants. Not that I don't wear my pants where they should be, not that, but I've learned the lesson in humility that Cantinflas has given me with his. A man in jail will be something else the day he stops feeling himself to be a braggart, a dominator, and a despot and begins to be what he really is: a sad Cantinflas who can't even maintain the spontaneity of keeping his pants on tight."

There's the sound of a shot close by. We all drop to the floor.

"That was a rifle shot," Fatso Tudela explains.

"How do you know?" Oscar asks.

"The voice of death is always a familiar one for detectives," David says.

"Detectives can't hear a shot without becoming solemn," Mister Alba says, completing the thought.

Toscano asks Mister Alba:

"Why do you say ladies and gentlemen?"

"In jail you never know who's who," Mister Alba says. "In a place where there are so many men who belong to the weaker sex, it's best not to stray. It's best not to wound any sensitivities."

He stands up and shows signs of wishing to withdraw, but before leaving he places a coin in Toscano's hand.

"Here's a tip, waiter," Mister Alba says, patting him on the back.

117

MONDAY, NOVEMBER 9

This city doesn't feel well; it feels like a criminal
who's thinking about his next terrible crime.
   D. H. Lawrence

8 A.M. Right on time, the men start filling up the cafés.
From the terrace I can count the cafés. As far as my eyes
can see there are eleven on the street directly across from
where the jail is and I am. At this hour, as if they were
gathering for some fateful conclave, men begin filling up
the cafés and the cafés begin filling up with the sounds of
the men. The sounds of conversations, promises, flattery,
business, intrigues, complaints.

The army tanks and police patrol cars still stand between
the cafés and the jail. They haven't moved since the riot
began. Personnel carriers from one unit or another arrive
from time to time. They discharge platoons of armed men
who replace those in the tanks and cars who, all tired out,
immediately get into the carriers and leave.

It's strange watching from the jail the men in the cafés.
At first sight it looks as if freedom is accustomed to being
spent in the cafés during the day. Under careful observation the men seem to be prisoners, too, fastened to the chairs
where they sit and the tables where they eat and drink and

chat. Although it's still quite early it's obvious there's no lack of people drinking cane liquor at this hour. Those who do it this early drink their liquor from coffee cups so that all is done in accordance with the strict demands of public morals. But most of the customers are drinking coffee out of demitasse cups, which, seen from a distance, steam like the smokestacks of toy boats.

The hours pass quickly in the cafés but the appearance of the establishments doesn't change with the passage of time. And the noise doesn't change either, always the same succession of sounds blending into the volume of the popular uproar. If it weren't for the fact that some men doubtlessly get up and leave, you could say that the people ensconced in the café were one and the same because they never change.

From the cafés the men look at the tanks, look at the patrol cars, look at the jail. That apparatus of oppression can't tell them very much. They turn to look at the jail. They write something on a piece of paper. They get up, go to the telephone, come back to their seats. They keep on drinking coffee in an effort to provide their nerves with the stimulant they can't get from the simple matter of ful-filling their role as free men.

Women aren't allowed in these dens of idle males. The lack of any feminine softness gives the cafés a genuine homosexual character. This aspect makes them resemble the jail even more. It also makes these establishments gloomier with their damp and steamy insides, much like a keg of warm beer. Women pass by on the street without looking into the cafes. There is an immediate range of avid necks stretching out toward the street like the necks on ventriloquists' dummies, trying to get a whiff of the aroma of the passing perfume. The necks on the alerted dummies are screwed back into their trunks, waiting for more passing perfume, making room in their insides for another cup of coffee.

As seen from the jail, the prisoners in the cafés turn out to be rather sad. They're living on small stores of sloth and illusion. They mumble and talk about things they don't understand, like war or politics. They subjugate and dominate the women they don't have. They put some miserable life into the death that's causing their knees to swell. When they're not slandering someone they're squawking and complaining about government taxes. They have their shoes shined incessantly until their feet catch fire. Embalmed in the smell of their coffee, these mummies of freedom present a very poor picture of it.

From time to time lottery vendors appear and enter the cafés. There's some secret and cynical complicity between cafés and the lottery. The vendors offer their merchandise of numbered hope to the customers' foggy eyes. They immediately invest in the ticket for the grand prize and then the vendors betray them by continuously hawking at the top of their lungs the winning ticket of the inexhaustible grand prize. The men in the café pocket the slice of illusion which will feed them hope for a week and excuse them from performing any work for the rest of their lives. Even if out of work they buy lottery tickets as if guaranteeing themselves the assurance of a life without work.

"I'd like to win the lottery so I could pay my lawyer," Mister Alba says.

The men in the café read newspapers, which they give the importance of a great cultural act. By reading the newspaper they feel like citizens of Athens. This tendency toward this most comfortable form of classicism and humanism is so marked that they feel called upon to call their little city the Athens of the Andes. They're happy feeling like Athenians as they read their newspapers in cafés. From the jail we contemplate from afar this curious caricature of Greek genius.

With regard to Athens and newspapers, the Honorable Fatso Tudela asks Mistér Alba:

"Were there newspapers in Athens?"

"Unfortunately no," Mister Alba replies.

"What about Socrates?"

"Socrates didn't know how to write. He was an oral philosopher like me."

"What did Socrates do?"

"When he wasn't a prisoner he spoke on the main square every day. In our time Socrates could only have been a radio announcer."

There are plenty of people who think that cafés are more or less disguised branch offices of jail. The ones who believe this base their opinion on the fact that among the tables of the cafés the usual drug dealers do their trafficking day and night as if on their own turf. This clandestine traffic reaches right into the jail, but it has its base in the cafés. In this way the cafés feed a little on the misfortunes of the jail. I can't look at a café without thinking of jail and without thinking about the iniquitous lifetime link that joins them.

Looking at the cafés in another way, I gradually start thinking about all the jail means to the small city. In some way the jail is the city's best defense. It's not the police but the jail that provides security and confidence to a man's life. What would this small city be without us? What would those cafés and that church and that drugstore and that school and that cemetery be without the prisoners? The men in the cafés and the ones who pray and the sick ones and the ones who study and the dead ones, all the men who are in some way free of the jail are compelled to be its tributaries. They work for it. They pay for it. They rest in peace for it.

Where there isn't a good jail, there isn't any good freedom. Justice and jail are the sum total of freedom.

121

10 A.M. There's a mezzanine in the café, a kind of platform with a wooden floor and glass walls, where the café manager lives and works. The manager is a fat young man whose paleness makes me think of the figure of Nero played by Peter Ustinov. The fellow goes about in shirtsleeves although he always wears a vest, a striped vest that he can't button up over his opulent belly.

In contrast to some of the customers on the floor below who drink liquor in cups, the manager up above drinks coffee in a glass. He lives between glass walls and drinks from a glass container as if to show that there are no secrets about his behavior. The hot glass burns his fingers but not his lips. He drinks the liquid with such satisfaction that you get the impression that the sound of the ravenous slurps reaches all the way up to the jail.

The owner is the sleeping synthesis of the café. He sits in a rocking chair all day long, taking his ease in that wooden shaker, drowsy in the back and forth of the chair's frustrated advance. On that carved wooden pedestal he spends his time drinking glass after glass of coffee and watching his belly grow. Down below other men are vegetating as they drink their coffee and there are others who serve it, intent on inflating that monument of cushioned buttocks in the rocking chair.

You have to recognize there are exceptions down below in the world of the café men. From time to time a man will pass right by the door of a cafe. This exceptional man, however, has the look of having come from a different café.

11 A.M. The students appear at eleven o'clock. From the terrace we watch them arrive. A short while before their shouts had announced their presence.

"It's a demonstration by the boys from the university," Toscano says right away.

The boys from the university, as Toscano calls them, number two hundred, more or less. They come in tight-knit groups with a kind of disciplined disorder, shouting and shaking their fists in the air. They also carry signs, which we can't read at first. When they reach the army tanks an officer orders them to halt.

We soon realize it's a demonstration in sympathy with the prisoners' protest. The students are demanding free passage to the jail. We can't understand what's urging them to come here. From a distance it looks as if they've organized a protest so they can be let into the jail. But the soldiers and police block their path and prevent their advance. Even so, they manage to reach a spot up front. Then we can read the signs they're carrying.

Although there are some rather specific signs asking for justice for the prisoners and the firing squad for Leloya, all the other writing on the innumerable signs makes us laugh. One says the Americans should stop their intervention in the jail. Another says "Down With US Imperialism!" Another proclaims "Yankees Go To Home!" The most difficult one to interpret, however, is a sign with the pharmaceutical symbol of death, a skull over two tibias, that reads "Jail or Death!"

When they're cut off, the groups of students become notably tamer. Some sit on the ground and take out their books. It's time for studying. Others settle in the café because they're already practicing the art of café life. Only a small group of extremists remains next to the tanks, asking to be allowed up to the jail. While they wait they keep on cheering for an end to U.S. imperialism.

"I wonder what would happen if they let them come here," I say to Mister Alba.

"Nothing would happen," he says. "The young never know what they want."

"But their gesture of solidarity with the prisoners is quite touching," the Honorable Fatso Tudela says.

"They take sides with the prisoners as a game so they

won't have to study and under the pretext that the jailers are oppressing the prisoners. With that aim they're just as capable in the same way of siding with the jailers, too, saying they're being threatened by the prisoners."

"You haven't got a very good opinion of our student class," Toscano ventures to say.

"I know youth, that's all," Mister Alba says. "Although I may not look it, I was young once myself. If I were the army I'd let them come. They're capable of getting themselves killed just to get here, but once they find themselves in the jail they won't know what to do with their victory, the same way that they don't know what they're fighting for. Read the signs they're waving in the air. Written signs are the intellectual flags of all revolutions."

We've stopped looking at the students and are listening to Mister Alba with the attention he demands of his audience when some shots ring out. We drop to the floor. At first we think they're shooting at us. We prisoners have our pride: we live waiting for them to shoot at us. But we immediately hear shouting in the street where the soldiers and police are shooting and the students are attacking or running, still shouting against imperialism. One of them can't run or shout, however.

His comrades pick up his body and carry it off with the blood flowing as they retreat.

The blood does nothing to eliminate the previous tension thereabouts. We can't see very much from the terrace. We don't know what's happened. David comes up from the courtyard and says the version circulating among the peasants is that six students have been killed.

"Today marks the end of the university for us," the Honorable Fatso Tudela comments.

"If it's not the end of the university at least the university's autonomy is finished," I say.

"What's autonomy?" Toscano asks.

124

"Autonomy is the art of turning universities into jails," Mister Alba explains.

"Let's proclaim the autonomy of the jail the way the students proclaim the autonomy of the university," David proposes.

A moment later David rectifies those somewhat hasty words to himself.

Oscar comes up from the courtyard and says that down there they're sure fourteen students have died in the street battle.

Without our being able to stop him we see David leap up onto the railing. There he clenches his fist and shouts:

"Murderers!"

From the towers they answer with a burst of machine-gun fire. They would have hit him if a moment before Mister Alba hadn't given him a strong whack on the knee. The blow makes him stagger and fall just as the bullets from the machine-gun bite into the wood of the railing.

"What kind of foolhardiness is that?" Toscano asks.

Another inmate who comes up from the courtyard informs us that the number of dead isn't fourteen but twenty-five. Following the orders Mister Alba gives us with his eyes we all remain silent. We all endure the danger to which David has just exposed us with respect and dignity. We've all understood David.

For a moment the blood of the old university student has boiled up in that man jailed for forging his uncle's checks. The students' support, which we can't understand, has just been returned from the jail with interest. The innocent victims have received the emotions of this prisoner who's just become excited and reckless with the madness and youth of a student.

4 P.M. Mister Alba calls me over to a corner of the terrace.

"I want to tell you something," he says to me confidentially.

"I'm listening," I reply.

"Leloya wants to negotiate."

"Leloya's acting very tame."

"We're no longer in the days when it wasn't necessary to consult before you squeezed the trigger. Military men with no autonomy to shoot make the best diplomats."

"What did you tell him, Mister Alba?"

"I let him know I'm ready to negotiate too, but under my own conditions."

"That's the way to talk. What are those conditions?"

"In the first place, instead of my going to see him, he comes to see me."

"He won't accept."

"We'll see about that. If he doesn't it will show he's afraid. Secondly, I've demanded that any agreement has to be made on the basis of the peasants going free as soon as the agreement takes effect. The term of their provisional detention is long past. There's nothing against them. It's an injustice to keep on holding them in jail."

"That's fine. What else?"

"They will have to guarantee that we will be able to use the courtyard every day for at least three hours. We can't go on not being allowed to take a few steps in the sunlight the way it's been for the last few weeks."

"That would be a natural follow-up to freeing the peasants. As I understand, it's because of too many prisoners in a jail not built to handle them that the regular outings in the courtyard were cut off."

"Finally, I demanded that no reprisals of any kind be taken against anyone, with the exception of Toscano, who they can punish any way they like."

"Why Toscano?"

"There won't be any evidence against anyone. But there'll be evidence against him. I'll say that he was the one who opened the door for me to take part in the riot."

126

"Toscano opened our door to help us," I claim. "It's not right to accuse him now, Mister Alba."

"That may be true, but you won't be accusing him. I'll accuse him. I'll take the responsibility for that immoral act before I'll take it for the crime down below in the court-yard where the peasants are dying of thirst and typhus. The water's run out. While Toscano was arguing about the legal aspects of the organization of the committee, in the courtyard everything the opposite of what I ordered was taking place. And after that my instructions about ra-tioning weren't followed. It's all settled. We need a war criminal to pay for the sins of all. Politics is like that. I've picked the scapegoat. It's Toscano. This legalistic thief is going to have a new opportunity to invoke the law in his favor. There's nothing else to be done."

"What's going on between you and Toscano, Mister Alba? It's best to be careful. Don't forget the prisoners of today can be the guards of tomorrow."

"I won't deny that I detest him, and I detest him because he's a black marketer who quotes the law. A black mar-keter is the worst kind of thief. He's the kind of thief who in olden days would have stolen with his feet so they wouldn't cut off his hands. In our times he's capable of robbing with his mouth so he won't leave any fingerprints."

There really wasn't anything else to do.

But I'm ashamed of the solution and it's considerably lowered my wavering notion of Mister Alba's generosity.

5 P.M. Fatso Tudela invites me to get to know Leloya, whom I've never seen before in my life. As he hands me the binoculars Fatso Tudela notices that my hands aren't too steady.

"You're shaking," he says.

"It's nothing," I answer.

I hold the binoculars and look toward the tower on the left. At first I can't see him. He has his face covered with his binoculars because at that moment he's looking at us, too.

"He's the one with the moustache," the Honorable Fatso Tudela says.

I can see the moustache quite clearly on the face emaciated like that of a dead man. According to the Honorable Fatso Tudela that pale skin is the result of Leloya's alcoholic excesses.

I see his eyes, a pair of frightened eyes, ready to flee, like the eyes of the rat. And yet they're hard eyes, with the look of porous bone or damaged cartilage about them. His legs hang down from his tiny body into a pair of wrinkled military boots, boots that hold swollen knees and twisted tendons. This man isn't content to be just an ugly dwarf. He's also gloomy and deformed. He looks like a character out of Goya painted by Picasso.

His hand is on his pistol. At that moment I wouldn't have understood the man if I hadn't seen him with a whip or a pistol in his hand. That man with a pistol in his hand doesn't terrify me. What terrifies me is that someday I might hold a pistol myself and therefore be like him.

I wipe the sweat from my brow with a handkerchief. Fatso Tudela looks at me uncomprehendingly.

"What's wrong?"

"I'm sweating."

"But you're all upset."

"It's nothing."

"Do you want to look anymore?"

"I've had enough."

"What do you think of Leloya?"

"I've had enough Leloya for today."

"Do you hate Leloya, Antón?"

"About the same as you. I didn't know him until today. Today I've seen him for the first time."

"That's enough, then."

"That's what I said."

"Would you like to kill him?"

I don't know why he asks me that.

9 P.M. The cafés near the prison square are still open. Four men in shirtsleeves who've been playing cards all day long continue their shuffling and dealing. They're prisoners, too, prisoners of gambling.

A tireless lottery vendor reaches the group. One of the gamblers is a man clinging to the idea of not missing a single chance. Not content with the card game, he plays the lottery, too. The other players look at him with disdain. They look at him as if he were betraying them.

Upstairs in his glass tower the manager is getting ready for bed. He's left the rocking chair to drop into a hammock that's hung from the walls by two iron hooks. No sooner is he ensconced in the hammock than it begins to sway, perhaps to rock him to sleep. The fat man who looks like Nero enjoys the movement until he falls asleep, as long as he doesn't have to move himself.

A woman passes along the sidewalk in front of the café. Beside the gamblers a man is lying in wait. At a given moment he follows her, approaches her. Properly arranged, the crime and the sin look like Chinese characters projected against the street wall by the lights of the café. There's something sadly sweet about that fortuitous love. Then both prostitutions are lost in the dark night of freedom.

But a moment later the two figures come into my angle of vision again. I get the feeling that I know the man. I look for the binoculars to identify him, but when I get the couple in focus it's too late.

All that's left behind are the leprous walls of a building. Over the main door I read: "Hotel Libertad, Speciality Beds With Netting." The only thing I can ascertain is that the man is bothered by mosquitoes.

In a corner Nancy is answering David's questions with his own voice.

"I love you, Nancy," I hear him say.

Oscar comes dragging along to a spot where there's obviously no danger but where he makes a great show of hiding from the invisible ambush. It can be seen that I've made a good impression on the renegade priest. Every chance he gets he looks for me to have a chat. He always talks to me in a penitential tone, as if he were confessing me.

"Aren't you going to sleep?" he asks.

"Not yet," I answer. "I like looking at the life of freedom from here."

"So do I. Especially at night. Looking at freedom from here is like looking at the world with your binoculars reversed."

"That's what I was thinking a moment ago. Looking at the street I felt the way a movie actor might feel if he was given the supernatural gift of watching from the screen the public that's going to watch him."

"What's the news?" Oscar asks.

"Mister Alba intends to negotiate," I inform him.

"He'll have to. It's a shame."

"Why is it a shame?"

"This has been a meaningless riot. It doesn't seem like a riot but more like a strike, a work stoppage."

"I didn't know that riots had to make sense."

"Not sense," Oscar says. "But they do have to have deaths."

"Deaths?"

"Yes."

"If they need to have deaths, then go kill somebody, Oscar."

"I've already done all the killing I've had to do. My quota of murders has been filled."

"Does a person have a running account of killings?"

"I know it because I've killed. You don't because you're innocent. But that's the way it is."

The word of my innocence had reached Oscar, too. At that moment my mouth fills again with a bitter taste. I begin to swallow the strange taste of innocence. It's as if a swarm of wasps was stinging me in the throat and filling my cries with the hot wine of their poison.

"The book of my dead will remain blank," I say.

"Nobody knows when fate might bring us to write something in it. Nobody knows that, boy," Oscar says, putting his hand on my shoulder.

Sitting on the floor, he then starts to unscrew his leg. Every night he takes his leg off to sleep. As soon as he separates it from his body he places it at his side and covers it with a blanket, as if it could feel the cold.

Then he hugs the leg. He squeezes it as if it were a woman. With a smile on his lips, hugging his leg with the tenderness of a child who clings to his favorite toy in the dark, Oscar begins to fall asleep.

A short while after he's asleep, I realize why he hugs the leg. Maybe he's afraid it'll be stolen. In jail anything can happen. Or maybe it's something more obscure. It might be that he's afraid that while he's asleep, feeling itself free the leg will start walking without him.

It's late and alone once more I look over the rather hazy outline of the small city.

Seen from the prison terrace at night, the city moves laboriously, as though it were lame. It moves in such a way that shows how the freedom outside would be castrated if the prisoners inside were removed from it.

At this moment, from the jail, the city looks to me like the ghost of the jail wandering around the jail at night.

TUESDAY, NOVEMBER 10

The Lord gave Cain the moon as a jail.

  Jorge Luis Borges

9 A.M. Leloya is just a few steps away from me. As if he'd been rejuvenated several years in one night, he looks much less old today than yesterday. Binoculars illuminate but they also age people.

There's no doubt that by his coming here Leloya has shown signs of incredible courage. It's part of the overbearing apparatus of his personality. In any case, Mister Alba ended up making him negotiate right where he wanted him.

A moment before Leloya appeared at the main gate of the prison. He comes unarmed, in civilian clothes, as Mister Alba wanted to see him. He goes through the courtyard where more than a thousand men who are his potential or declared enemies surround him. He goes step by step as if guided from a distance until he's beside me.

Although I'm sure he doesn't know me, he gives me a look of disdain. It's just his way of looking at other people. There's an unceasing mad and fateful flow of rancor at work between us. For my part I hate him as if hate had been invented just so I could hate him. I think I'll have to kill him so as not to go on hating him this way.

133

"Where's Mister Alba?" he asks me.

"He's waiting for you. Come with me."

"Just a minute. Where are we going to meet?"

"In the office. The two of you will be alone and you'll be able to talk without any interruptions."

"It wasn't established that we'd talk in closed quarters."

"I don't think it changes the terms of the agreement. It'll be better for the both of you."

"All right," Leloya says. "Let's go."

He has no way out now. I walk along in front of him. On the stairs, instead of heading for the terrace we go into the jail's main office, which, as been said, lies in the territory controlled by the prisoners. The floor is littered with scraps of paper, the remnants from the destruction of the first day when the prisoners got rid of the files, burning everything in them in the courtyard bonfire.

Mister Alba doesn't greet him.

"All right, Leloya. Let's begin."

Mister Alba signals with his head and I leave. Outside hundreds, thousands of eyes question me with an inexplicable urgency. I have nothing to tell them about the fate that awaits all of us.

10 A.M. I've finally just found out who the man is that the flies annoy. I've identified the man who was waiting for the appearance of a woman in the café last night beside the gamblers.

I'd thought about it all night long without being able to shed any light on the mystery. I became obsessed with that stranger whom I didn't recognize at first and who, nevertheless, left a spark of unconscious suspicion in my mind after he disappeared with his companion into the fly-proof Hotel Libertad. When it all came out the suspicion wouldn't let me sleep.

I don't know why I hadn't noticed it before. I almost feel tempted to correct what I've written down about the street scene with the mercenary couple.

There's a good reason for my not having guessed it at the beginning. During the day Ramírez wears rimless German glasses, the glasses of a scholar or a doctor. At night he takes off the glasses along with his title. Transformed into a man, he sits by the door of the café in wait for passing pleasure.

At night the man who promised me my freedom is out hooking hookers.

11 A.M. I promised to interrupt Mister Alba at this time.

When I get to the door Leloya and he are still there as though they'd been comrades all their lives, sitting on the only desk to have survived halfway the disaster of the first day. I don't dare put in an appearance. I wait for them by the door where Mister Alba finally sees me. He immediately calls me in.

"Come here."

Everything happens so swiftly that I'm unable to understand it myself.

"Escort the colonel to the street door," Mister Alba says.

"The colonel's staying here," I say.

"What?"

"I say that the colonel's not leaving here."

"What's all this?"

"A kidnapping."

"What's going on?"

"All I've got to say is what I just said. From here on Colonel Leloya is kidnapped."

"Are you going to ask for a ransom to give him back?"

"I haven't thought about that. In any case, he's been kidnapped."

"Who decided this?"

"Me. Antón Castán."

Those two words baffle Leloya. He rubs his eyes as if he can't see. The bundle of arrogance that arrived there two hours before was now a liquefied mass of quivering gelatin in a refrigerator with no power.

"What the devil are you up to, Antón?" Mister Alba asks.

"You heard. Leloya's not leaving here. He's our prisoner. A prisoner of the prisoners."

"I'm in charge here. I had him come here. I've negotiated surrender with him. We'll do what I say."

I immediately speak up. I do it calmly, not so much in order to convince Mister Alba as to complete Leloya's demoralization.

"Outside there are a thousand men waiting for my orders. They've all agreed to hold Leloya. You'll have to choose between Leloya and us, Mister Alba."

That's all that's needed. What surprised me is that it was so easy. Mister Alba shows no hesitation in believing what I'm saying. For him at this moment there's no doubt that everything was set up outside between the prisoners and me. The last doubt keeping him unsure disappears when Leloya says;

"Your betrayal has been perfect, Mister Alba. But if you don't release me it'll go hard on you. If I don't get back to them my men have orders to machine-gun the prisoners."

He still has the will to consider himself the master of our fate. He's still counting on the men waiting for him. I tell him:

"Your men may fire on us but they'll also be firing on you, because as of right now you'll always be in front of us."

"Why are you doing this?" Leloya suddenly asks in a plaintive tone.

136

I answer him with four words that explain everything to him:

"Because I'm Antón Castán."

Before I can dodge Leloya leaps up and punches me in the face. It's a good punch, I have to admit that. It knocks me down. Before I come to my senses and get up Mister Alba is already showing signs of being with me. Breathing deeply, he opens the curtain of fat on his belly, unsheathes the straight razor, and places it at Leloya's throat.

I get up and go out. I call the members of the steering committee.

In one respect at least things immediately return to their previous state. Mister Alba starts giving orders again.

"We've decided to hold Leloya. Antón will make arrangements for guarding him. Obey him the same as if I was the one giving the orders."

I give orders to Toscano, Fatso Tudela, and David at once for them to guard Leloya and I leave the office accompanied by Oscar and Mister Alba.

As I look around I can understand at that moment up to what point a man can sense collective feelings on certain occasions. For once in their lives these prisoners wanted to give themselves the luxury of having a prisoner of their own, a prisoner to bring before justice. I'd guessed their thoughts and I made Leloya a prisoner.

3. P.M. Outside, the students have organized another demonstration. There are a lot more of them today.

At the head of the group they're bringing the boy whom we took to be dead yesterday as a symbol. He has his head wrapped in gauze and bandages and leads the march of the groups with the mechanical prudence of a man who'd been brought back to life and was afraid of dying again. Of the six, fourteen, twenty-five dead that had been mentioned

137

yesterday, the only one left is this rehabilitated wounded man, unhesitatingly followed by his comrades. I'm not interested in the students anymore. I've started tiring of what's going on outside the jail. I'm beginning to be weary of that freedom of foolish shouting, remunerated love, tragic indolence, grotesque sufficiency. I'm surprised and pained by that world which I've been given to look at of late and which my eyes, old after three years in jail, almost no longer can recognize.

Of everything I've had to do today, the easiest has been convincing Mister Alba of the reasons for holding Leloya. Mister Alba accepts them without any great objections. I think he's doing it because, as I see it, Mister Alba isn't used to feeling terribly comfortable when he has to play the role of a man who feels obliged to keep his word.

5 P.M. It's after five in the afternoon and nothing that everybody was afraid of has happened.

When Leloya didn't return at the time he was supposed to, his men contacted Mister Alba. They notified him that if Leloya didn't return by five o'clock they'd bombard the prison, move against us, and attack us with flame-throwers. In a very decisive way Mister Alba let them know that they could do it but that it would cost them the very worthy life of their colonel.

Five o'clock goes by and nothing, not a thing of what has been threatened, happens. At this time all danger of any violent reprisals has vanished. Night falls. From here on night will work for me.

Relieved by another prisoner in guarding Leloya, the Honorable Fatso Tudela comes over to me and shakes my hand.

"It was a good job, Antón," he says. "You've got the makings of a leader."

"I had to do it. How's the prisoner doing?"

As I use that word I feel a bit ashamed, not so much for Leloya but because where there's a prisoner there's a jailer. And in this case for the first time in my life I'm not the victim, I'm not the one being persecuted, I'm not the prisoner.

"He's as deflated as a bladder pricked by a nail," the Honorable Fatso Tudela informs me.

"What's he done?"

"He's asked for a priest."

"Well, then, he's afraid he's going to die."

"He's not afraid, he knows he's going to die," the Honorable Fatso Tudela states.

10 P.M. Oscar's getting ready for sleep. He begins by unscrewing the leg from his body. He's covering it with the blanket when I make him the strange proposition.

"I need you to lend me your leg tonight."

"What?" Oscar exclaims.

"Just that. I want to take your wooden leg."

In the shadows of the terrace his eyes, lost in the jungle of the tangled hair of his beard, seek mine out anxiously.

"What are you going to do, boy?"

"We haven't got any weapons. The wood of your leg is the only thing we've got available tonight to guard the prisoner with."

"The prisoners captured three rifles the first day of the riot. They've also made spears and clubs out of the broken furniture."

"Unfortunately, while we were arguing with Toscano about the legal aspects of the organization of the committee, the peasants were loyally turning over the weapons and instruments for battle to Leloya."

"Why did they do that?"

"They thought that in that way they could avoid any complications for everybody."

"All right, take my leg."

As I touch it Oscar's leg starts turning into a club.

It's made of oak and so sturdy and heavy that I don't see how Oscar can move about with that appendage attached to the stump of his leg.

According to what the Honorable Fatso Tudela has said, Oscar made the leg himself without ever getting to smooth it when he lost his original leg, threatened with an attack of gangrene.

In a hospital in an Andean village, the same veterinarian who'd cut off his leg fixed up the wooden replacement later on. He adjusted it as best he could within the means at his disposal, both orthopedic and equine. According to the Honorable Fatso Tudela, in spite of everything the job was a fine combination of carpentry and surgery.

I take the leg and place it on my shoulder as if it were a rifle. On the floor, missing a leg, Oscar looks as inoffensive as a wounded animal. I leave the terrace and start down the stairs, heading for the office with Oscar's leg on my shoulder. Oscar follows me with his forlorn eyes, like some mutilated animal.

11 P.M. Once again I find myself close to Leloya. Toscano and two other men are with us. I tell them:

"All right. You can all go and get some sleep."

"I'm not tired," Toscano says. "Taking care of Colonel Leloya doesn't tire me. It's like watching over a dove."

Toscano doesn't insist. I watch him go up the stairs to the terrace, followed by the two prisoners who'd been with him.

I count the seconds with my heart. For half an hour Leloya and I just look at each other without saying a single word. With every second that passes he seems less sure of himself. Suddenly he kneels down in front of me.

"What are you going to do?" he murmurs softly.

"My name is Antón Castán."

"Why don't you kill me right out?"

"My name is Antón Castán."

He starts to cry. He cries in a very strange way. The tears not only pour down but climb up his face as well. His forehead is covered with tears. He becomes aware of the role he's playing and swallows his tears with impotent rage. But he can't get rid of them. Fear is greater than all the insolence, all the cruelty, all the infamy this man has accumulated in his life of a mad dog.

Now he stops crying and starts speaking. He doesn't talk like a man but like a woman. This reminds me of my father's secretary in the jail he was in charge of, that man who didn't speak with the sinew of men's words but spoke with the liquid of women's tears.

"I'll speak before all the prisoners and all the guards and all the judges. I'll tell the truth. The whole truth. Nothing but the truth. The truth at last."

"My name is Antón Castán," is all I say.

Oscar's leg is implacable in my hands. Its annihilating blow has the ferocity of a lightning bolt that shatters an oak. As I hit him I think that if I can't spare his life I'm not going to spare his death either.

When I go out I breathe in the night air, but without any calm. I remember then that in a similar situation the Lord gave Cain the moon as a jail.

I feel free, with a freedom that overflows my body, with a morbid contentment that throbs within me in a strange way. Nevertheless, I understand that from now on, wherever my steps take me, I can no longer be free with that happy and relaxed freedom that comes with innocence.

Still carrying the homicidal club, I understand that with what I've done, God has just broken away from me. I understand that the Lord has just given me life as a jail.

III
The Trial

SATURDAY, NOVEMBER 14

I have an immense advantage over you no matter what you do;
I have killed.

Georges Simenon

Ever since last Wednesday we've been locked up in our cell again.

It's a bit strange they didn't decide to separate us after all that happened. Just the opposite, once we decided to halt the uprising, give ourselves up, and renounce all demands, the first thing they did was to call in Mister Alba, David, the Honorable Fatso Tudela, and me. All of us together as though we had rights of reservation to the cell, we were returned to it without their asking us anything. They didn't even search us when we went in.

That business of not asking us anything is even stranger. Right up until today no one has asked about anything that took place in the office. It looks as though one dead man more or less no longer matters to anyone in this country.

Once they had us locked in our cells they set free the peasants. Then they picked up Leloya's body and took it away. Everything turned out so natural for everybody that, according to Mister Alba, nothing would have surprised the guards more than finding Leloya alive in the place where they found his corpse. His men could foresee that Leloya might die. Why they let him go to his death knowing it could happen or, even more, knowing it had to happen, is something we still haven't been able to understand.

It only took a few hours for the jail to go back to its prescribed normality. Wednesday night a guard told us that a civilian official had just taken over the management of the jail. No sooner was he sworn in than he sent for the guards and ordered them to use humane treatment with the prisoners. No punitive measures or authoritarian excesses. He announced that he was going to run the jail like a school and he made it clear that under his administration everybody should be prepared to pay more attention to order than to punishment.

It must be true that our future is laid out on these plans because yesterday we got back the right to go out into the courtyard. They're not giving us the three hours of courtyard that we had before. They tell us that from now on we'll only get two hours a day. In any case, this daily escape from the bleakness of the cell is almost like winning back all the joy there is in the world. They say that when things get completely back to normal we'll have three hours a day in the open air again.

Yesterday during our first outing since the riot I ran into Oscar in the courtyard. His pant leg was modestly covering his wooden leg as if Oscar had something shameful to hide. My hands still burned from that wooden leg.

"How goes it, Oscar?" I asked him.

"Getting used to peace again," he answered.

"What cell have they put you in?"

"I'm in a common barracks. The cells are for the prison aristocracy."

"How many prisoners are there in the barracks?"

"Sixty."

"Ask them to give you a cell."

"No. I'd rather stay in the common dormitory."

"The common room is a dung heap."

"Yes, but a cell is another jail inside the jail. I can't take a cell. I get claustrophobia. A cell's like being condemned to drink blood from the heart of the jail."

Oscar is absolutely right, of course. Still I prefer a cell. As I see it, it's mostly because of my cellmates.

In the courtyard yesterday I also ran into Toscano. As soon as he saw me he came over with the face of a dog that's been beaten but is still treacherous.

He began to describe for me as best he could, with a luxury of detail, the spectacle of Leloya's corpse, as if he wanted to shock me. I wasn't listening to him but I couldn't escape that mistreatment with words that kept pecking like a flock of crows at the shapeless mass of broken bones and mangled flesh.

To my great surprise Toscano wasn't talking about it to bring my troubles back to me as I'd first thought. I discovered that when he suddenly said to me:

"Look at Mister Alba there. He's getting ready to witness the reconstruction of the crime. Or maybe he's only asking permission to go into the office. I'm beginning to believe it's true criminals like to return to the scene of their crime."

As a matter of fact, Mister Alba was standing by the office door chatting with a guard.

Toscano went on:

"I never would have thought that Mister Alba would dare do it."

"Do what?" I asked.

"Kill Leloya."

"So was it Mister Alba who killed him?"

"You know better than I."

I knew, good God, how well I knew. And yet those words of Toscano's as they arbitrarily moved me away from where I belonged also gave me a touch of relief.

Neither at that moment nor now can I accept the suspicion that Toscano was interested in making it appear that Mister Alba was responsible for Leloya's death. And yet, given the animosity between the two and Mister Alba's opinion of Toscano, anything Toscano said about Mister Alba could also be believed. I remembered a prisoner I'd seen in the jail a long time back. He was a poor devil, a bit loony. Only in jail could it have occurred to that poor devil that they'd stolen his crime from him.

Sentenced for a crime that obliged him to spend two years in jail, he decided because of money and through the influence of I don't know what obscure machinations to exchange identities with another prisoner. After two years the other one got his freedom back and this fellow stayed in jail paying for the crime of the one who'd swapped with him. When he found out that he'd have to spend eleven years in prison for a crime he hadn't committed but which he'd taken on as his own, the man started to go crazy. They'd come across him in the courtyard looking at the sky and repeating over and over:

"Give me back my crime... Give me back my crime..."

Toscano continued:

"Everybody in the jail knows it was Mister Alba who did it."

"How do they know?"

"Mister Alba doesn't deny it."

"Does he admit he did it?"

"He says he's ready to declare he did it."

"Did he tell that to you?"

"Not to me, no. I'm not one of Mister Alba's favorite saints. But in the courtyard he's told it to anyone who wanted to listen."

148

I've thought a great deal about what Toscano told me yesterday. I don't think Mister Alba's generosity has reached the extreme of letting himself be accused of something he didn't do just in order to save me. I know how his feelings work but I also know how his mind works. His mind is a calculating machine. His penetrating calculations are limited to preventing through a kind of automatic guessing game any reaction good or bad that might be produced by life in jail.

I immediately discard the idea that Mister Alba wants to be the hero of Leloya's death for the jail. Murder has no place in the rich collection of his crimes. Not even for reasons of prestige does a crime of this type fit into Mister Alba's psychology, much less his taking on the fame for a killing without having killed. His connection to the crime is less resonant but more reproductive.

I know, therefore, what Mister Alba is after with this. By accepting or encouraging versions that attribute Leloya's death to him, he knows that without compromising himself too much he'll be contributing to the dismissal of my responsibility and will be moving me away from it. His tactics would also see to it that if a witness might accuse me, in the remote case that this witness might appear, a lot of other witnesses, it's not known how many, would be ready to lead the testimony astray if it gets closer to the truth.

I'm sure that Mister Alba doesn't want me to be accused. He's hoping that Leloya's death will be considered a natural consequence of the uprising, an act of collective agreement. Something like an act of war, for which individual responsibility can't be ascertained.

In some way Mister Alba has succeeded in this intent up till now.

As for myself, I know what's happened. I know what's right for my conscience in this matter.

149

But as a prisoner in a jail where I'm not alone, I know that everybody shares or is condemned to share my responsibility, if I have any, or my remorse, if I come to have any. It's as though all of us prisoners had agreed to share among ourselves, in quotas of minutes or hours, the payment for the total time that legally corresponds to the expiation for the crime.

On the other hand, I don't feel very sure of myself as I tread the slippery ground of the crime. When I killed I felt free for having killed. Now I'm no longer convinced of having lost my freedom when I entered the jail. Now I think I lost it the moment I killed.

In any case, as far as I'm concerned, the crime belongs to me. For the jail, the crime is collective. It's such a poor crime that it holds no secrets for anyone. At the same time, it's such a rich crime that it holds punishment for everyone.

SUNDAY, NOVEMBER 15

I, too, belong to these prisoners and prostitutes.
   Walt Whitman

The humanitarian and sanitary measures laid down by the jail's new warden begin to be applied quickly. From today on we have to bathe twice a week, Wednesdays and Saturdays. It's obligatory and done in groups. But we'll also be able to bathe on other days if we make individual requests to that end.

Starting today we'll also have three hours a day in the open air. In order to avoid dangerous groupings like the ones that brought on the last riot, there will be three successive shifts daily to go out into the courtyard. We get the first one in the morning, which begins at eight o'clock.

At eight o'clock we go out together with all the prisoners from the section where our cell is located. They move us along the hallway in Indian file. Each prisoner carries a towel and a bar of soap. Even though it's cold the prisoners are wearing just their pants. In the hallway the long line of naked torsos is shivering with cold.

In the courtyard the morning sun is shining on the place where an improvised shower has been set up. When the riot began the angry prisoners destroyed the booths made of branches where the prison baths were set up.

The new installation is nothing but a garden hose connected to a faucet in the inner courtyard and tied to a post. The end of the hose shoots a spurt of water over a raised platform. The naked prisoners have to pass one by one under the flow and bathe and soap themselves in full view of everyone. This brings out protests by Mister Alba.

"I never thought we'd come so low," Mister Alba says.

"It's the prisoners' fault for ruining the booths."

"No matter what, this is an unheard of humiliation."

"Would you rather not have a shower?"

"I like to bathe, but to bathe alone or in good company. This business of doing it in public in front of this entourage of scoundrels takes away all the charm from the act of bathing."

"We're part of the entourage of scoundrels. Besides, nobody's going to stare at you."

"It's not a question of whether other people stare or don't stare. It's a question of my feeling uncomfortable."

"Bathing was worse in Dostoyevsky's day," I state.

I start telling Mister Alba about Dostoyevsky's baths. In his best-known book, *The House of the Dead*, Dostoievsky describes bathing in jail. It's a scene right out of Dante, filled with noxious vapors and the incredible fluids of decomposition. The reader comes away from the bathing scene with his soul afoul. I speak to Mister Alba about this scene and he shows a great deal of interest.

Now it's getting to be our turn to bathe. As they approach the hose the prisoners take off their pants and leave them on the ground. Then they get under the shower, leap about, sing, and soap themselves as they drip joyfully under the caress of the cold water. They come out all jolly, drying themselves and going back to pick up their pants.

Near the shower there's a guard who plays the role of master of ceremonies for the bath. Pointing out the path they're to follow, he keeps on repeating:

"Don't push, gentlemen, don't push. There's water enough for everybody, gentlemen."

He calls us gentlemen as if it were the most natural thing in the world. His way of describing us seems to have its effect. At least for a moment, hearing themselves called gentlemen, the inmates stop pushing and mouthing foul language.

The scene has the melancholy charm of merry things that are sad. No one can escape being the target of double-meaning jokes. Mister Alba can't accept any of it. For him that exhibition is not much more than a market in slave flesh.

"That fellow Dostoyevsky wrote quite well," Mister Alba assures me, trying to separate himself in his mind from the spectacle surrounding him.

"He's one of the greatest novelists in the world," I state.

"He liked to write about prisoners."

"About prisoners and criminals and the sick and the persecuted and idiots."

"More or less about the people who fill the jail. That's why I like him."

"You like Dostoyevsky? He's very human but very bitter."

"I like human writers who are bitter. I like strong dishes, raw red meat, à la Dostoyevsky. What I don't like in literature is the flowery stuff. I prefer my roses in the salad."

Mister Alba stops because it's our turn. Mister Alba goes ahead of me. From behind, without any pants on, he looks more like an old woman than an old man. No sooner does he take off his pants than a man in back of us, as though the one who'd just undressed before his eyes was a beautiful woman, gives out with a lewd whistle. That infuriates Mister Alba but he can't do anything because nobody knows who whistled.

When he starts soaping himself I get under the stream of water.

"Careful of your tattoo," I warn him.

Mister Alba rubs himself vigorously. The effort brings on a cough. His body isn't exactly fat but robust, although in his case there are quite a few extra pounds of fat on his belly.

Under the shower again, he starts to jump. A moment later he gets ready to dry himself off.

"Do you remember Raskolnikov?" Mister Alba asks

"He's one of Dostoyevsky's best-known characters," I say.

Putting on his pants, Mister Alba says:

"I've always wondered what would happen if Raskolnikov were living in the Russia of our time. I'd like to know if he'd join the Communist Party."

"They wouldn't let him in," I say.

"Because he'd killed?"

"Because he felt free after he'd killed."

After bathing, one by one, we pass into the hands of the barbers. The barbers protest because it's hard to cut wet hair, but they have no recourse. The law's the law. The rules of the jail mention bathing first and haircut after. These details have great importance here because, as the guards say, when it was arranged that way it must have been for a good reason. According to the guards the legislators know what they're doing.

There are four barbers who don't use scissors or combs but a shearing machine. The barbers work at an incredible speed. In five minutes they turn a prisoner out without a single hair left on his head.

Mister Alba observes:

"This business of getting our hair cut from time to time has its good points. As far as I'm concerned the barber is useful in reminding me that I have a head. After my hair's been cut I feel rejuvenated, as if the barber had just pruned my tree of knowledge."

After the three hours of our shift are up we go back to the cell. David and Fatso Tudela follow us. After bathing Fatso started playing soccer so that now, all sweated up, he gives the impression that he hasn't bathed at all.

In the cell Mister Alba gets paper and pencil and starts writing. David and Fatso Tudela play chess. I write, too.

At this moment I feel that in the cell all of us are free.

The wonderful thing about jail is that it reveals unsuspected secrets about different, complicated, unknown forms of freedom. At this moment I feel that our prisoner bodies have, nonetheless, autonomous zones, free parts. Our mouths, for example, are free now because we're silent. On the other hand, in jail the freedom of not listening doesn't exist.

Mister Alba comments:

"We can write in peace, Antón. David and His Honor have just locked themselves up in the concentration camp of the chessboard."

"What are you writing, Mister Alba?" I ask.

"It's a secret."

"A diary?"

"That's what you're here for. Don't worry about any competition."

"A novel?"

Mister Alba doesn't answer. He continues writing imperturbably. Every so often, in order to write something, he consults his confidential file. I'm intrigued by Mister Alba's attitude. Without knowing what he's writing, by the mere fact that he's writing, I feel a little displaced by him on the level of intellectual importance. In literature there's nothing worse than finding out that others can do better what we think we're doing well.

For a moment David leaves the chessboard concentration camp. He looks at Mister Alba and comments:

"Another writer?"

"So it seems," I say.

"The only thing bad about jail is that it stimulates literary inclinations," David says.

And he locks himself up in the chessboard again.

"That one thinks that writing is a heroic deed," Mister Alba says, referring to David.

"For my part writing isn't just nothing," I state, "Writing is living."

"For me writing is like loving," Mister Alba says. "Writing for me is lifting up the skirt of words. It must be painful to be imprisoned and not know how to write."

Mister Alba sighs, whether for the skirts or for the words isn't known. In any case, it's as if deep in his heart he felt what he's saying. He goes on writing but lifts his head a moment later and asks me:

"Between Tolstoy and Dostoyevsky, which one is greater, Antón?"

"They're both giants," I reply.

"They're both giants, no doubt about that, but they can't be equal. What's the difference between one and the other?"

"Tolstoy is a mirror on the path," I say. "Dostoyevsky is something more. By himself Dostoyevsky doesn't need a mirror. Dostoyevsky is the path."

Mister Alba tells me that he doesn't feel well.

"It's the bath."

"It could be."

"Take an aspirin."

156

Mister Alba looks at me calmly and says:

"I'm not an original as a man, but I'm very original as a sick person. Ordinary remedies don't work with me. Bicarbonate gives me indigestion and aspirin gives me a headache."

MONDAY, NOVEMBER 16

I am a man, therefore I am an accomplice.
  C.G. Jung

We're in the courtyard at sun time. We call our turn at leisure sun time even though quite frequently at this hour there's no sunshine in the courtyard. Today is precisely one of those days. High dark clouds cover the light as if up in the sky God was trying to hide from us behind a screen of threatening darkness.

David and I are sitting on the stone sill. We're away from the rest of the inmates, most of who are watching the soccer match taking place in the courtyard.

Nearby a centipede has fallen to the ground. It waves its useless legs upward, treading impotently on empty space. Its ineffective extremities keep kicking in the air as its paralyzed body is unable to straighten out and move along the ground.

David says to me:

"Look at that creature. It's got a hundred legs but it can't walk. Mister Alba would probably say that it's a true picture of freedom."

In the soccer game things are going along differently. The players' feet are moving as fast as they can go, turning

158

this way and that, behind the ball. And yet, the fact that they can move and run doesn't let the players lose their status of prisoners. Quite the contrary, the more they move about on the soccer field the more they seem to be prisoners, slaves of the frenzy that they themselves are chasing with their feet and which they follow with their whole body, undismayed.

David isn't very communicative today, one might say. I ask him:

"What's wrong?"

"My Uncle Apolinar died," he says.

"I didn't know."

"I don't like to talk about those things in the cell. He died last week."

"Was he very rich?"

"He was rich. And he was a strange character. Like so many people who persist in falsifying themselves, my Uncle Apolinar wasn't really a man but a character in a play. He was the Christianized embodiment of avarice. That was what brought him to turn me in. As far as I could tell he only owned one suit in his life. But he always wore it clean and perfectly ironed, except that he had the pants pressed wide. The pleats weren't at the front of the legs but on the sides, which gave him the look of a clown."

"I would have liked to have known him."

"He had the notion that everything was better in the past and when he spoke about ancient justice he would say that, first of all, crime had to be humanized. By humanizing crime he meant doing away with revolvers and going back to daggers. Among his friends he had the reputation of an atheist. One day I asked him if that was true and he told me: 'I'd like to believe in God but God won't let me.' Now, at his death, he's pulled off the greatest joke of his life. In his will he disinherits his honest nieces and nephews and leaves me his whole fortune. In the will he says something like: 'I leave all my possessions to the son of my sister María, David Fresno, my nephew, who is now in jail. I do not leave them to him because he is my nephew or because he is in jail but because David, being the only relative who tried to rob me in life, is no longer interested in robbing me after I am dead.'"

"Congratulations," I say. "With that inheritance you won't have any worries when you get out of jail."

"The worries have already started. The disinherited relatives have already demanded that the will be nullified, stating that my uncle was insane."

"He must have been from what you've told me about him."

"If he was, I'm going to prove that he got his sanity back to make the will."

In spite of everything David doesn't seem too enthusiastic about the inheritance from his uncle.

In order not to freeze we walk a little among the prisoners watching the soccer game. The referee is the Honorable Fatso Tudela. Fatso is a strict referee. Every two minutes he blows the whistle, calling the players to order. As he imposes the corresponding penalty, this convict referee takes on a superior, almost majestic air.

Many years ago when I was a schoolboy, certain national customs were inspired by models from the most erudite times of classical antiquity. In our school, for example, one soccer team was called Sparta and the other Athens. Here in the jail we don't go back so far. In names at least, we're up to date. One of the teams playing today is called Chicago and the other Stalingrad.

These names don't correspond to political leanings in the jail. They are instead, imposed by the environment and the moment. "Stalingrad" is made up of thieves and swindlers and "Chicago" by gunmen and murderers.

160

Past the courtyard where they're playing we bump into Mister Alba. He sees us pass but doesn't say anything. He's involved in throwing dice. Crap games are prohibited in the jail, but Mister Alba is a master at not letting himself be caught breaking the rules. One day a guard discovered him and as he approached the group playing he had the great surprise of seeing that the men were acting as if they were playing but playing without dice. The guard could see that they were fooling him and he became furious, searching them one by one. But Mister Alba had made the dice disappear, using one of his usual tricks. In the presence of the surprised guard the prisoners continued playing without dice, but mimicking all the action of a real game.

I tell David:

"Mister Alba is a hard-core gambler."

"I don't like that word, Antón," David replies. "Hard-core is a ridiculous word."

"I didn't know there were such things as ridiculous words. All words express something more or less. That's their job. That's why they're words."

"They all express something, but there are some that are ridiculous. Using them in writing is a serious fault, but using them in conversation is a crime."

"Could you give me examples of some ridiculous words?"

"All literary words have something ridiculous about them. Listen to some of them. Hard-core, tempestuous, astounded, upstanding, opulent, faraway. In jail you can't say faraway. In jail there's no beyond."

"When you come to think about it, you might be right. In any case, Mister Alba likes to gamble. When he's not shooting dice he acts as if he's shooting dice. And on his days outside he plays the lottery."

"I can't stand the lottery. Buying a lottery ticket makes me feel I'm part of a herd I don't belong to because I'm an accomplice in something that's unsure. I bought a ticket once and tore it up before the drawing. I can't bear the prospect of getting to win the grand prize. Ever since then I've detested the lottery. Waiting for the lottery is like going to bed with the fear of finding a snake between the sheets."

"You've said prospect and detest. Now I understand your theory. Prospect and detest are two ridiculous words. They're like old-maid words, words that haven't found their destiny."

"I won't use them again."

"Does saying that you don't like the lottery mean that you don't like money?" I ask.

"I like money, Antón. I'm in jail because of money. But money disturbs me. I'm afraid of it. I know it because I've stolen it. What I don't like is linking up human illusions to something as dirty as money. Fortunately there are still people who don't believe in the lottery. In Usaquén a lady won five million of the grand prize in the Christmas drawing. A reporter asked her how she felt. She limited herself to answering, 'I don't believe in luck.' That's called having a sense of honor."

"Honor is another ridiculous word," I observe.

David says:

"The other day in a letter from Nancy I saw the word honor written without the first letter. Without an H, Nancy's 'onor' didn't look like honor but like a poor mutilated sin. That day I discovered something important. I discovered that for human civilization, matters related to pride and morality aren't based on a person's conscience but on proper spelling."

TUESDAY, NOVEMBER 17

Virtue is a horrible thing; it's the opposite of freedom.
  Virgil Gheorghiu

In the middle of the afternoon three guards armed with rifles open the cell door. One of them announces to us:

"A delegation of Catholic ladies is coming to interrogate you. Although you can tell them whatever you want, the only thing the warden wants is for you to answer them with all politeness, as if you were real gentlemen. In any case, we'll be right here to keep order."

I recognize this guard as the one who called us "gentlemen" as he led us to the shower. It's obvious that he's a very mannerly man and that the word gentlemen produces a pronounced psychological effect on him.

A moment later three aged ladies reach the cell door. One of them is carrying several folders in her hand. Another carries a notebook and a pencil. Of the third we can only guess the importance of her personal authority emanating from the surface of her skin. All three look like stuffed parrots, lifeless scarecrows that still retain some color. The guard's demands were unnecessary because these ladies are the type of women who can't fail but to bring out gentlemanly reactions in men.

"Good afternoon, gentlemen," the three say in a chorus.

"Good afternoon, gentlemen," Mister Alba repeats, echoing them.

In spite of the hilarity this arouses in the Honorable Fatso Tudela, this first contact between the two groups creates a rather uncomfortable situation. In order to erase the bad impression of the reply, Mister Alba decides to alleviate the tension by comporting himself like a gentleman.

"We are at your service, ladies," he says in a ceremonious tone.

The head lady says:

"We are a working group from the Society of Friends of the Prisons recently established and with branches all through the country. We are making a survey of the situation in jails. We are asking you for your cooperation."

"We are at your orders," David also volunteers.

"The first question is quite simple," the chief lady says. "We want to establish the limit of responsibility corresponding to prisoners in the existing social order. Along these lines I'm going to put a concrete question to you. Do you people know who killed Colonel Leloya?"

"What does Leloya have to do with the social order?" David asks in turn.

But the Honorable Fatso Tudela interrupts him to state:

"I can speak with authority in this matter. With my experience as a detective I've made an internal investigation of this. I can inform you that Colonel Leloya committed suicide."

The lady with the notebook begins to write. With every word she raises her eyes, consulting the one in charge of the interrogation. The latter continues:

"That version of the facts doesn't satisfy me. It's incomprehensible that Leloya would want to kill himself when everybody knows that the only thing he liked was killing other people. They already told me about that suicide business in another cell. But, after all, clearing up that matter is a job for the police. For our part, we're only interested in social matters. Let's move on. We've found out that mysterious graffiti have appeared in several cells of the jail, crude drawings that look like swastikas. This has led us to believe these signs are directly related to the Jewish question. Could you people tell me what the prisoners think about the Jewish question?"

"Excuse our ignorance, but what is the Jewish question?" the Honorable Fatso Tudela asks.

The lady asking the questions doesn't know what to answer. A wall of suspicion and nervousness has arisen once more between the two groups. Mister Alba hastens to clear up the misunderstanding.

"As far as the Jewish question is concerned," he says, "the only thing we know is that among the prisoners there's a money-changer that some call the 'Syrian' and others the 'Jordanian.' He's involved in loans for buying and selling at the modest interest rate of forty-nine percent. In other words, the jail Arab is so rapacious that he acts like a Jew."

The lady with the notebook is taking notes without a pause. It's clear to see the course the interrogation is following isn't to her satisfaction.

Taking advantage of a pause, the lady with the leaflets starts passing them out to us. I take the one she gives me and look at it. It's entitled:

"Cigarettes and Cancer."

"Instead of bringing us cancer you should have brought some cigarettes," Mister Alba says.

"We're educating people, not promoting vices," the lady says shrilly.

"Fine. I'll smoke the pamphlet," Mister Alba concludes with resignation.

The one asking the questions puts an end to this mock battle by asking further:

165

"Could you tell us if it's true that there's been some communist infiltration in the jail?"

"There's been no infiltration here except for the leaks in the ceiling of the cell," David says.

"Why do you want to know if there's any communist infiltration?" Mister Alba asks.

"Because if there's communist infiltration there won't be any more American aid."

"What does American aid for the jail consist of?" Mister Alba asks.

This time the lady shows her discomfort. She looks at her companions. The one with the pamphlets, who's the most combative, says:

"We've come to interrogate you people, not for you to interrogate us."

But Mister Alba still asks:

"What does it consist of? Can you tell me what American aid for the jail consists of?"

"Maybe they want to install an electric chair here," the Honorable Fatso Tudela suggests.

"Don't answer. You're not obliged to answer," the lady with the notebook advises the lady doing the questioning.

But the latter shows herself to be conciliatory. She states with great conviction:

"I can't give an exact answer, but I imagine it's some kind of Peace Corps activity. They only want to hold out their hand to us. They want to help us build a new world, one that's more humane, more democratic, freer. In a word, they want to teach us how to live the way they live. As far as jails are concerned, they want to help us build jails where men can feel free and not like prisoners."

It wasn't too clear, but for a moment her speech touches us. The lady who has just spoken has obviously succeeded in clearing up a sticky situation. Taking advantage of her success, she goes on to the next question:

"I should like to know your tastes in reading matter. I can see you're allowed to have a lot of books. That's what we call culture. Do you like the poetry of the great classic Nuñez de Arce?"

"Generally prisoners don't like bad poetry, much less that of the great classics, and still less that of Nuñez de Arce."

This was abruptly stated by the Honorable Fatso Tudela, but it didn't upset her.

"Speaking of human relations, do you people read Orison Swet Marden?"

"No!" David replies. "What do you take us for? Do you think we're North American prisoners?"

"In economic matters what school do you prefer?"

"We have no preferences in economic matters. But speaking of schools, we only belong to that of Master Vargas Vila."

The lady with the pamphlets crosses herself with her free hand, as if Mister Alba had just named the devil.

"What?" the one with the notebook asks.

"I said that speaking of schools, we follow the school of Master Vargas Vila," Mister Alba repeats condescendingly.

"That monster?" the lady says, crossing herself again. The situation is now more volatile than ever. Nevertheless, the one in charge of the group once more makes use of the intelligent tactic that has proved so successful, changing the subject.

"The Society of Friends of Prisons is very interested in knowing what solutions you prisoners can propose for the common problems of the country."

"For that," I indicate, "Mister Alba has a special formula."

"What special formula is that?" the lady asks.

"Let's talk first about the common problems," Mister Alba says.

"What, in the opinion of the prisoners, is the most serious problem facing the country?"

"The devaluation of the currency," Mister Alba states.

"What formula do the prisoners have for it to recover its value?"

"As seen from the jail, the problem is quite easy to resolve," Mister Alba assures her.

"How?"

"By changing the name of the peso."

"What name would you suggest for the new monetary unit?"

"The peso is weak because it's called a peso. If instead of being called a peso we call it a dollar, its power will improve notably. Besides, it would sound quite nice to talk about the Colombian dollar."

"The United States will protest," the lady says. "They've patented the name of the dollar. But, in any case, the Society of the Friends of Prisons will study the matter. Make a note of that, Madam Secretary," she orders, speaking to the one involved with the notebook.

She pauses and then says:

"Well, then, the last question of the survey is the following: Is there a need for reforming the structures of the jail?"

"With all due respect," Mister Alba says, "what are those structures?"

Undoubtedly the reformers don't know what the structures are. In view of the deadly silence brought on by his question, Mister Alba takes the easiest way out:

"We'll support the reform of structures. Those two words, reform and structures, promise a lot."

The visit of the working group is concluded. The ladies begin their withdrawal but not before the lady with the pamphlets tells the one doing the questioning:

"There's one question left."

"Which?"

"The one about charity."

"That's right. How much are the prisoners prepared to contribute for the maintenance of charity?"

"We are prepared to contribute to the maintenance of charity the same amount that charity will contribute to the maintenance of the prisoners," Mister Alba says.

"Thank you for your polite collaboration, gentlemen," says the well-mannered guard, locking up the cell.

WEDNESDAY, NOVEMBER 18

A man who has a dog on a leash is just as much on a leash as the dog.
  Antonio Birlán

As I go about watering the flower, Mister Alba asks me:
  "Has the rose bloomed yet?"
  "No, but it will soon."
  "When it blooms it's not going to bloom with rose petals but with wire spikes."
  "In any case, it will bloom. I'm sure."
  "I've got my doubts that wire can bloom."
  "Before it was wire, many centuries ago, this stem belonged to the vegetable kingdom. It wouldn't surprise me if it also belonged to the mineral kingdom. I'm watering it centuries late, but it will bloom someday. It's a matter of patience. Have no doubt, Mister Alba."
  From one surprise after another, the Honorable Fatso Tudela has just learned about this other bit of madness in the cell. He can't believe his ears or his eyes. But he doesn't reject the fiction. The Honorable Fatso Tudela has an advantage in that nothing in the jail surprises him. As far as I can see, it's just as if he'd been with me ever since the first day of my three years in prison. Maybe because he was a detective Fatso acts as though he'd been born in jail.

170

A corporal dressed in civilian clothes comes to inform David that permission for him to leave jail for a day has been granted. The corporal adds that he'll accompany him and dressed like that, in civilian clothes, no one will notice that David is a prisoner on furlough. David had put in a request to visit his family two days earlier. He didn't expect them to let him go, although from what he told me the new warden was a friend of his. And he evidently was.

The corporal also announces that we won't be going out to the courtyard in the morning today because of some special circumstances. But he promises us that we'd enjoy our approximately three hours of open air in the afternoon.

David feverishly gets ready to leave. He gets dressed in a hurry, putting on his best clothes and since he hasn't got any decent shoes I ask the Honorable Fatso Tudela to let him have Braulio's temporarily, the ones the latter had left behind in the cell. Fatso says sure and that in exchange he has a favor to ask of David.

When David's ready, he asks us all:

"What would you like me to bring back?"

I ask for two books and His Honor asks him to phone his wife. David takes down the name and address that Fatso dictates to him on a piece of paper. Mister Alba has nothing to request.

When David leaves Mister Alba says to Tudela:

"I didn't know you were married. You don't have the face of a married man."

"Does marriage give you a special face?" Fatso asks.

"Yes."

"What does it look like?"

"Like your face."

Fatso Tudela tells us about his wife. Judging from the picture he paints of her for us she must be a good woman. Of course, women are just a pretext for him to talk to us about his former profession of detective, which was the only thing of interest to him when he was free.

"When I get out I'm going back to being a detective," Fatso states.

"If they rehabilitate you, you can be a detective again," Mister Alba notes.

"Will I have to be rehabilitated? I didn't kill because I liked to."

"Nobody kills because he likes to. In your case, if they rehabilitate you it means that they're rehabilitating you to go back to killing."

"Why do you like being a detective?" I ask.

"I like to put people in jail."

That's the only answer Fatso gives. Mister Alba comments:

"David's lucky. I never thought they'd give him permission."

"The warden's a relative of his," Fatso comments.

"Not a relative, a friend," I clarify.

"It's the same thing," Fatso says. "Relative or friend, he gave him permission. I'm sure that if I asked they wouldn't give it to me."

Mister Alba observes:

"What gives us the nature of prisoners isn't our status as such, but the guard who keeps watch beside us. In the street today nobody will take David for a prisoner. When he leaves with the corporal the two of them will look like a couple of brothers out for a stroll. When I'm free and walking on the street and I come across two men who look like brothers, I'll immediately be suspicious of them. I'll think that one is a prisoner and the other his guard."

"He's a nice fellow, that David," the Honorable Fatso Tudela generously confesses.

"That's right. He's got a fine hand," Mister Alba says.

172

"Fine hand?" Fatso asks ingenuously.

"Yes. He writes very well. Especially when it's a case of writing bad checks with his uncle's signature."

"I don't like to say bad things about a person when his back is turned," Fatso declares.

"I do," Mister Alba assures him. "A few pecks on the back of my neighbor is a restful thing for me, it gives me a good feeling. Everybody does the same thing. What happens is that I'm not a cynic and I confess my predilection for backs, or my cowardice when it comes to backbiting."

For a while I spend my time watching the main courtyard through the window. In the courtyard I see a group of prisoners who look like the peasants who started the riot. There's no doubt that they're peasants but they're not the same ones. These are even more miserable than the others. They're barefoot and in their thin white clothes their bodies are shivering from the Andean cold.

Looking at them I understand now that these peasants are the "special circumstances" the corporal was talking about when he told us that we wouldn't be able to go out into the courtyard this morning.

When I leave the window Mister Alba and the Honorable Fatso Tudela are still talking about David. Fatso says:

"Well, yes, and talking of writing, David is very proud of what he's writing."

"But he never writes."

"He says he writes and that he writes very well because in his town they speak very good Spanish."

"Believing they speak very good Spanish is the only consolation left to people who speak Spanish."

"Don't you believe what David says?"

"No."

"Why?"

"Everybody who speaks Spanish speaks the same as all those who speak Spanish. No one people speaks better Spanish than another."

"But why?"

"Because there's no such thing as good Spanish."

"What about in Spain?"

"In Spain even less. In Spain there are those who write well, very well, of course. But the ordinary Spanish of Spaniards is almost worse than the ordinary Spanish of Spanish Americans. Just read a translation from any language into Spanish and you'll see what I'm talking about. There's nothing more provincial than the Spanish in translations. Spanish translations are a triumph of slum talk added to a triumph of verbal poverty. In them characters from Balzac talk about paying the café bill with *perras gordas*, fat bitches, Spanish slang for one of their coins. In the same way Mexican translations call Gide's boys *chamacos*. In the ones from Argentina they'll say that the evil Raskolnikov is a *malevo*. Argentine and Mexican translations are Spanish America's revenge for Spain's translations."

At two o'clock they take us out into the courtyard.

The yard is full of peasants from the hot regions. With clothing that wasn't meant for the climate here, the altitude of the Andes is making them shiver from the cold as if they were suffering from malaria. They look like migratory birds from the tropics lost in the high mountains.

These peasants are quite different from the peasants we met before in the prison courtyard. Those came from the Andes and were more like human beings. Their sadness, which they also had because sadness among peasants is like a family trait, was less depressing. Those were peasants from the cold highlands, involved in growing wheat, barley, and corn, which are the crops of men. These now, on the contrary, come from the lowlands, from the valleys

174

of the tributaries of the Magdalena, of which the Spanish conquerors spoke. Their servitude is more abject than that of the others. They plant sugar cane, which is a crop for slaves; they plant tobacco, which is a crop for addicts; they plant coffee, which is a crop for beggars; they plant rice, which is a crop for pariahs. In other words, while the peasants from the heights of the Andes grow bread, like men, the peasants from the lowlands grow money, like gamblers.

These twin social groups have nothing in common except poverty and ignorance. Neither one nor the other has any redemption. The land makes them what they are. The torrid zone makes them lazy, the frigid zone makes them indifferent. Both are the human face of earthly tragedy. At this time peasants are nothing but a picturesque curiosity in a landscape.

When I ask them why they were arrested they tell me that guerrilla bands attacked the lands where they were working. The ones the guerrillas didn't kill were arrested by the police. They explained that they were bringing them to the jail in order to protect them, but they were really jailing them as a way of showing that they still held authority over the peasants, which they didn't have over the guerrillas. Since they hadn't been able to take the guerrillas, who had killed, as prisoners, they had to content themselves with the peasants, who hadn't let themselves be killed.

In the courtyard Toscano gives us the big news:

"Have you heard the latest? David escaped."

"What?"

"Just that. David Fresno escaped at noon today. He got away from the guard who was watching him. A girl helped him escape, taking him off in a Ford."

That detail about the girl is enough to remove any doubt from people's minds. We all recognize Nancy as the girl in the Ford.

After the first moment of surprise, each of us comments on David's escape in his own way.

"I never imagined him capable of doing that," the Honorable Fatso Tudela says.

"Freedom's getting to be so bad outside that it's taking away the function of the jail," Mister Alba declares.

I'm perplexed. I can't explain why David didn't let me in on his plans for escape.

After three long hours roaming about the courtyard, talking about the peasants and the escape, we go back to the cell. To our great surprise we find David there. The first thing he does is hand me the books and tell the Honorable Fatso Tudela that he spoke to his wife. His Honor pats him on the back and shoulders several times to make sure he's not a ghost. David asks for an explanation.

"They told us you'd run away," I say.

"The one who ran away was the guard."

"The guard?"

David explains to us that while he was with Nancy the guard got drunk and sold his revolver so he could keep on getting drunk. Then he took off. Tired of waiting for him to come back, David decided to return to jail alone.

"Nancy brought me in the Ford," he finishes.

"Since when has Nancy had a Ford?" Mister Alba asks in turn.

So he won't get into a quarrel with Mister Alba, I ask David to tell us what he found out about the state of affairs in the country.

"The guerrillas are still robbing and killing," David assures us.

"They've been at it for fifty years," Mister Alba states. "Now they say they're being led by Communists and financed by drug traffickers."

"What about the Army? The police? What are the forces of law and order for?" I ask.

This is what Mister Alba says:

"The guerrillas are well-armed, therefore they're dangerous. As far as the forces of law and order, as you call them, are concerned, it's better for them to keep watch in jails, where the prisoners are unarmed. By taking care of prisoners, the forces of law and order haven't got time to go up against the guerrillas."

Then David starts talking about Nancy. He tells us what he spoke to her about. His voice is filled with Nancy. His lips are swollen from Nancy's kisses. I've never seen him as happy as he is today. If we had a moon tonight David wouldn't spit at it this time.

Then one of those unforgettable dialogues takes place in the ivory tower of that cell as two confined intelligences snap back and forth with the crack of a whip.

David recalls Nancy:

"We had lunch together at her house. The table was decorated with onion flowers, white flowers that have the virtue of giving a touch of aroma to your appetite. We ate chicken along with some Spanish delight. Nancy uncorked a bottle of Rioja wine, a warm, thick wine that tastes like butterfly blood."

"One moment please, could you tell me…" Mister Alba starts to say.

"What butterfly blood tastes like?"

"I know that quite well. In the Amazon region I got drunk on it many times. Drinking butterfly blood is like drinking a rainbow stirred in a blender. Butterfly blood is a liqueur of colors, like the wings of butterflies. I don't need you to explain what that taste of colors is like. No. I just want to know, in all humility, what Spanish delight consists of."

"It's a dish based on Italian macaroni, Argentine ground beef, and Venezuelan corn. It's a typically Colombian dish, Chinese in origin, and popularized by Americans under the name of Spanish delight."

The day has been so agitated that in order to sleep I've had to whistle up the dead. I fall asleep counting the dead, who arrive one by one, jumping through the bars of the cell.

THURSDAY, NOVEMBER 19

In prison I spent the most fruitful and freest times of my life.
  Jawaharlal Nehru

After spending several days trying to write something, Mister Alba has dramatically given up being a novelist. After revising, rereading, scratching out, and writing again, only to erase it once more, he's finally recognized that his intellectual life doesn't reach beyond being a market-place orator or an insuperable jail-cell conversationalist. With ill-concealed fury Mister Alba burns his ships in front of everyone, tearing up all the pages he's been working on for a whole week.

As a way of apologizing to me for having let his failure show, Mister Alba agrees to have me look over the surviving pages of his thick confidential file. There are some items he holds back for unknown reasons, although explicable in a man as complicated as he. The rest he hands me without hesitation. They make a rather thick pile, which I read with growing interest and quite rapidly.

The bundle contains notes, paradoxes, thoughts, fallacies, a whole philosophy of suffering and cynicism accumulated and marinated in various jails and over many years of crime and captivity. The greater part of the material, although showing much talent, is nevertheless unpublishable. Mister Alba is an author for men with more than forty years of jail behind them. But there are some items in the confidential file that are reasonably acceptable and worthy of being shown and preserved.

The following selections of famous statements by Mister Alba share a common vertebrae. That's why I save them for insertion in the diary, with great satisfaction on my part and with the benevolence of the author. This is because the thread that unites these ideas is the theme I'm obsessed with myself: freedom, justice, jail.

"I can't understand how Braulio Coral has been able to survive two marriages. A man who gets married is a man uprooted from himself. Getting married is cutting off our family tree at the roots."

"In jail the birds hate Oscar. With his Marxist beard and his wooden leg the birds don't see him as a man but as a scarecrow."

"In jail there's no greater lie than the truth."

"Why can it be that when we kill we never remember that we're Christians?"

"Rome is a lesson in balance. It teaches us the Law but it also teaches us how to wield an ax."

"The warden underwrites the contracts for feeding the prisoners, keeping a commission of ten plus ten or twenty percent for himself. His accomplices call this an operation in higher mathematics. Higher mathematics is the art of demonstrating how one hundred is one hundred twenty, minus ten, plus ten, or twenty percent."

"For a man condemned to death there's nothing more comical than the executioner's death certificate."

"David Fresno says I'm a cynic, but I don't think so. Cynicism can only flourish in freedom. Two examples of cynicism are given by an executioner who lets himself be hanged and a woman who cheats and puts horns on a bull-fighter."

"It's easy to be a criminal. But there's nothing harder than getting to be a prisoner. A small slip-up in the investigation, a subtle sophistry on the part of a lawyer, a correct or a skewed interpretation of the law and the rich possibility of jail is destroyed. A prisoner isn't exclusively a man who's committed a crime. A prisoner is a man who's stayed free of the police."

"God is a democrat. He doesn't retain power for himself but distributes it through a benevolent ministerial trinity, Father, Son, and Holy Ghost, who give us bread, freedom, and miracles. Don't fight with God, prisoner. God is three distinct persons. It's an uneven battle."

"Jail is the proof of freedom. I'm free, therefore I can be a prisoner."

"I don't know of any more stupid bit of hypocrisy than that of writers who write the word whore by putting down the first letter and follow it with four dots. Those immoral moralists have left us with the sin but without the pleasure. The golden age of Spanish literature corresponds to the period when writers wrote out the whole word. The period of decadence of the Spanish language is the age in which writers decided to shave off the last four letters of the word. That's the difference between a Cervantes and a Ricardo León. For the genius, prostitution is nothing less than a human humiliation for all who call themselves such. For the classic, prostitution is reproductive trade that only shames those chosen. An academic is incapable of writing the word whore. Cervantes isn't. I'm with genius and truth, that is, I'm with the whole prostitute."

"In moments of depression in here I think that our homeland is the place where we're free to say bad things about other people. From time to time, though, gusts of human solidarity also reach the cell. I understand then the grief of the exile, because then I understand what a homeland is. A homeland is not being alone."

"What is justice? The rabble that saved Barabbas? The court martial that condemned Dreyfus? Justice limps, but it gets there too late. According to Antón Castán justice walks so slowly that it grows old along the way. When it gets there nobody recognizes it because it arrives changed into injustice. Justice is like the Chinese warrior who was fighting for the the life of an emperor whose dynasty had ended a thousand years earlier."

"*In My Prison Time*, Silvio Pellico states that in jail they could shoot a prisoner without consulting the emperor, but in order to cut off the gangrened leg of a prisoner they of necessity had to consult the emperor. Pellico also tells us that the emperor was very sentimental. He had hundreds of political prisoners, but he became quite sad when he saw a prisoner. This reminds me that before I landed in jail I also knew a sentimental cop. Across from a building under construction he was shooting at a worker up on a scaffold. After shooting him, the cop covered his ears so he wouldn't suffer from the sound of the body when it splattered on the law of gravity's cement."

"I know how to live with little, and of the little I need very little, Saint Francis of Assisi said. I know how to live with little and the little I need I know how to get, says Pitigrilli. I know how to live with little and the little I need I know how to steal, said Antonio Toscano."

"We have to read the books prohibited by censorship, by all censorship, not in order to judge the worth of the books, but to appreciate the stupidity of all censorship."

"Man is a prisoner who runs away."

"The shield of Colombia says: 'Freedom and Order.' Freedom and Order is a perfect patriotic motto. In jail it's translated this way: Freedom to kill first and Order to run away after."

"Papini says that words are the prison of poetry. In search of the poetry of freedom I let my thoughts wander along an imaginary road and everything I come upon along the way suggests an instrument of oppression. The yoke of the ox team. The barbed wire of the farmer's seed bed. The channel of the river. The straight-jacket in the hospital. The rifle of the sentry. The whip of the horse breaker. The school of the boarding student. The rein of the horse. The street of the pedestrian. The city of the citizen. Everything is oppression. The steering wheel of the car I'm riding in isn't free. If it were free it would only be good to make the car crash. The picture they take of me isn't free. If it were free I'd be able to escape from the picture. On the road the arrows that show the freedom of movement also mark the great restriction of the freedom of traffic: they indicate the prohibition of moving backward. I finally come to the church and at the door I leave behind my road jailer, my guardian angel. Here at last I feel free. The church is the only place where a man is completely free and that's because in church the jailer is God."

"There are no prisoners in detective stories. In detective stories there are only fugitives. Jail puts an end to all mysteries. A fugitive is a prisoner who still hasn't run up against the truth."

"The drama of justice consists of the fact that the freedom to kill carries with it the freedom to hide from the police and the freedom to lie to the judge."

"I detest proverbs. Yet there are some that in jail make me think. He who runs with the wolves learns to howl. This proverb shows the force of evil. On the other hand, you can't speak of the force of good. He who walks with the innocents isn't infected with innocence. Innocence can't be taught or learned."

183

"Jail walls bother me. Did they build these walls to protect freedom from the threat of the prisoners or, on the contrary, to protect the prisoners from the dangers of freedom?"

"In any case, I can't deny that I suffer from the voluptuous quality of these walls. If the vagabond's homeland is the sun, my homeland is the jail."

"In jail, where reading Marx was forbidden, Oscar preached a sermon against communism. The eloquence of the renegade priest was so compromising that it inspired the idea of escaping from jail in order to read Marx."

"In jail I begin to get interested in freedom. Freedom carries the germ of prison in itself. To be free is like galloping on a merry-go-round. You're in constant movement; you're almost flying from so much movement. But you can't get off the merry go-round horse without risking falling onto the jail floor."

"The defect of prison reform is the fact that it's always in the jail and never in the prisoner. Prison reform proceeds like the near-sighted critic who in front of Goya's painting is moved by the sofa and forgets the Naked Maja."

"A brave prisoner is a man too cowardly to run. In jail being brave is not keeping your feet in place."

"In a jail in Panama I met an American who dreamed of having an escalator for climbing trees. He said that only in that way could he get back to nature."

"The jail clock doesn't seem to have been built to tell time but to set off an explosion. The jail clock has an ominous sound. It has the sound of the clock in a time-bomb."

"Ever since the rat died the jail has been full of spiders. We'll go hunting tonight. We'll organize a safari to go after tarantulas."

"They said that Mercury had one cold breast and one warm one. Gracián speaks of the woman who had one cheek full of life and the other cheek full of death. In Cartagena de Indias I met a mulatto woman who was the most beautiful symbol of racial integration: she could get along with anybody, north and south, east and west, because she had one white breast and one black one."

"Weep as we weep in jail, where both day and night are reserved for weeping. That's what Oscar Wilde said. In our jail writing is our way of weeping. Writing is weeping over our impotence. In our jail writing is a silence full of mute words wet with tears."

"The only completely democratic accomplishment of humanity isn't the common grave but the common cell."

"In the cell reading and sleeping are my occupation. I sleep where sleep finds me. I read where the book finds me."

"Antón Castán makes me think that a prisoner who writes a book is never innocent."

"I knew a man sentenced to 220 years in prison. I feel sorry for that poor man, condemned to immortality."

"The guard justifies the prisoner in the same way that the priest justifies the sinner. The guard is a prisoner who's locked in the cell from the outside. His civil service career is the guard's life imprisonment. The jail is a river with a bridge and the guard is the bridge and the prisoner the river."

"In the jail there's a prisoner who shows that America is for Americans. His hair is of the white race. His blood is of the blue race. His eyes are of the yellow race. His lips are of the black race. His skin is of the green race. This man of the Americas has not a family tree but a family forest."

"From the cell I keep watch on half the world. Even though I'm a lynx, I'm a one-eyed one. I see very deeply and I see very far but I only see half of it all."

"In jail we have time for everything. We have so much time that we even have the luxury of killing time."

"Antón Castán is the jail chronicler. Seen in another light, he's the poet of artificial flowers."

"In man, freedom is God's trademark."

FRIDAY, NOVEMBER 20

Apart from the murders he'd committed,
Burke was a very decent man.

George Mikes

It was very early when we get the news of Oscar's death.

"What did he die of?" I ask the guard.

"Old age," the guard explains. "He was sound but he wasn't safe. They found him dead in his bed this morning."

"Will he be buried today?"

"He's already been buried. Prisoners have got to be buried right away."

We don't understand why the guard is telling us this. It's one of those mysteries of life we can never get to the bottom of. When the guard leaves, Mister Alba talks about Oscar with the Honorable Fatso Tudela. The latter asks the question that's always asked among us about a comrade whose name has been mentioned.

"What was he in for?"

"For chewing gum."

"Is chewing gum a crime?"

"No. But if you use the gum to stick emeralds to your

beard and smuggle them into Venezuela it must be a crime because that's what they put him in here for."

"The least we can do is leave the dead in peace," David requests.

Mister Alba said that Oscar would get it into his head to travel to Venezuela very frequently. Sometimes he said he was going there to study the folk music of the Táchira region. Other times that he was going there to look up a brother who'd emigrated to Venezuela in the days of the dictatorship of the Most Worthy Juan Vicente Gómez. All those trips began to look suspicious to the police of both countries. They grabbed him in San Cristóbal along with his Venezuelan accomplices. It came out then that Oscar was taking Colombian emeralds into Venezuela through the simple procedure of hiding them in his thick beard, sticking them there with a wad of chewing gum. Busy examining his wooden leg, which is a highly suspicious item for a smuggler, the police ignored Oscar's beard, which was a nest of emeralds carefully wrapped in the matted hair of that male attribute of his.

Mister Alba sits down, writes a note, calls the guard, and tells him:

"Please take this to the warden."

When the guard leaves we're all waiting for an explanation of what it's all about. Mister Alba gives in to this obvious but unexpressed desire.

"I'm asking the warden to bury Oscar without his wooden leg. I'm suggesting to him that he build a monument to the unknown prisoner in the main courtyard. What I mean is the unidentified prisoner. There's no better symbol for the monument than Oscar's wooden leg."

I don't say anything, not because of my connection with that leg, but because for the first time I seem to discover in Mister Alba's head something that's not working too well.

188

It seems to me that David, too, is thinking the same thing. I don't say anything. I observe Mister Alba. I find that his face, lined with pits of cadaver paleness, matches my supposition perfectly. But the crisis reflected in his face doesn't last too long. Mister Alba goes back to talking about Oscar.

"He was just an ordinary prisoner. He won't go on to immortality."

"No prisoner ever goes on to immortality," states the Honorable Fatso Tudela.

"Your ignorance is touching, but it doesn't surprise me. The jails are full of prisoners famous in the history of humanity."

"For me, the only famous prisoner I know is the Count of Monte Cristo," Fatso says.

Mister Alba crushes him with his look and says this:

"It doesn't surprise me that your knowledge hasn't managed to go beyond the mental backwardness of Dumas Père. I'm going to give you a lesson in jailhouse history. Distant prisoners, in the most varied circumstances, all tied in with the evolution of human thought and feeling have among their numbers Socrates, Saint Peter, Dante, Galileo, Cervantes, Servet, Moore, Napoleon, Robinson Crusoe, Dreyfus, Dostoyevsky, Gandhi, Malaparte, Albizu Campos. And may other famous prisoners I can't mention now forgive me, because I'm not giving you statistics at this time of more or less immortal and more or less literary prisoners. And I won't mention those who died in jail. I only want to call your attention to the fact that the fame of certain prisoners is closely related to the obvious uselessness of jail as punishment. They put Silvio Pellico in jail and in his cell he became a monk, which is the height of piety because that's going a bit too far along the path of mortification. They locked up Oscar Wilde and during his

confinement he wrote his jail ballad that was the façade
with which his genius mind tried to disguise the vices of
the flesh that continued growing but no longer called out.
They killed Caryl Chessman several times and they
pardoned him several others, only to discover after each
frustrated attempt at elimination that his tender
murderer's heart was ever more hardened in crime.
Immortal prisoners show that jail serves no purpose at all
or a very small one. Jail is only a solution for those who
can't read or write. It doesn't correct their soul, but it clears
their mind and educates their hand because it teaches them
how to read and write."

I interrupt him:

"One objection, with all due respect, Mister Alba.
Robinson Crusoe wasn't in prison. Quite the contrary, he's
the strongest proof of the independence of the spirit and of
human freedom."

"Robinson Crusoe is a proof of freedom for other people.
For himself he's the most miserable of prisoners. One
day Robinson arrested Robinson and confined him to
an island. If that voluntary isolation, if that vocation for a
penal colony doesn't constitute the highest expression of
the jail spirit that we all have within ourselves, I don't
know what freedom is and I don't know what jail is."

The Honorable Fatso Tudela mutters philosophically:

"Let's drop the subject. I'm getting bored talking about
prisoners."

"What would you like us to talk about?" I ask.

"Let's talk about jails."

Mister Alba doesn't have to be coaxed. He talks on with
his customary eloquence:

"The names of jails have always fascinated me. I know
a jail in this country called La Concordia. I know another
called the Model Prison. That sounds ironic: concord and

model, two words of love and example. Still, in this matter we're way behind universal jailhouse poetry. Listen to this string of precious stones made up of the most famous jails in the world: Devil's Island, Regina Coeli, Auschwitz, La Santé, Ocaña, Nuremberg, Sing-Sing. Aren't your souls moved by such beauty?"

David asks him:

"What would you have them do? Do away with jails? Decent people have got to protect themselves."

"You hit it right," Mister Alba states. "When there aren't any decent people there won't be any jails. You can be sure that in the future there'll be a world without jails."

"What about criminals? Will all men be criminals? Will you leave this world open to criminals?"

"There won't be any criminals either."

"Will men turn good overnight?"

"No, but the concept of what's good and what's bad will change."

When arguments like this start up in the cell they never end. I begin to read until it's time to go out into the courtyard.

In the yard David asks Mister Alba to have a look at the part of the diary I'm writing they're unfamiliar with. So when we get back to the cell I start reading aloud. I read up to the previous chapter. When I get through my eyes are burning, not so much from all the reading as from certain parts of the work that deal directly with my way of taking care of Leloya.

"The part about Leloya's death is fine," Mister Alba says. "But the reader will want to know something more. He'll want to know why you killed Leloya. That's really the most important thing in the whole book. The reader will enjoy Leloya's death, but he's going to find it a little premature."

"The reader's going to have to be satisfied with what I've written and the way I've got it written," I say.

"Could you let me get to know the first part?" asks the Honorable Fatso Tudela.

"You'll have to wait till the book is published. Besides, the first part won't interest you, you're not in it."

Since David hasn't offered an opinion, I ask him:

"Do you like it?"

"Yes. But the star of the book isn't you, it's Mister Alba."

"The star is our cell. Personally, I'm not trying to be the leading actor," I state.

"As for me," Mister Alba says, "I've improved notably in the last few chapters. I don't look like a clown anymore but like a talking philosopher. This more recent picture does me justice, at least, because it moves me closer to reality."

David points out some small mistakes in the action that I promise to correct. The Honorable Fatso Tudela asks me to put a little more emphasis on his hopes to be reinstated in the corps of detectives when he gets out of jail. I also promise to do that, although David lets him know that for this it would be better to get a recommendation from the warden.

But the one making basic critical objections is Mister Alba:

"That business of quoting a phrase by a different author at the beginning of each chapter seems to me to be a little too much cultural pedantry or a sample case full of good literary connections."

"It's just the opposite for me," I maintain. "It's a gesture of humility aimed at reinforcing my convictions about freedom with the opinions of eminent men who've also written about it."

"If I were you I'd eliminate the quotations and stay all

by myself. It's better to be alone than to be in bad company."

"Haven't you said that you didn't like proverbs?'

"I don't like them. I despise them. That's why I use them. Using them is my way of despising them."

"In any case, I'm not dropping the quotations."

"Why do you insist on that whim?"

"For one simple reason. I just feel like it."

That must be sufficient reason because Mister Alba doesn't insist.

The Honorable Fatso Tudela notes:

"That fellow Braulio Coral who had the place I'm filling in the cell now doesn't seem to be a person of much brilliance."

Mister Alba answers:

"Braulio's place that you're filling now is a seat in the balcony. We've reserved it for the public that applauds. It's a place for a squire. The privilege of being geniuses we've divided among the three of us."

David adds:

"Braulio Coral was no shining light, I recognize that, but he had drawing power, the miraculous ability, that is, to attract and tame what bullfighting men and women have in common. Do you people know what Braulio managed to do when he got out of jail? Toscano told me in the court-yard. Something incredible. He succeeded in bringing together the two women who'd accused him before and got him into jail. Bigamy has borne fruit. Now he's living with both wives. And besides that, they're both very happy sharing his love."

With his habitual sarcasm, Mister Alba gets back to the criticism of what he's just read:

"As far as I can make out, a more complete book than this has never been written. According to the author it's history in diary form. According to David it's a play, like life, where we all do a little acting. According to my opinion, which is by no means a humble opinion, it's a novel. Maybe it's all of these. Maybe it's none of the three. But the work has a final advantage over others. After what Antón is writing today, the book will give us another bit of originality. It will carry its own literary criticism in itself. In this way it will put out of work those cannibals who in magazines and newspapers and between sips of Colombian coffee feed on slices from the skin of other people's corpses."

SATURDAY, NOVEMBER 21

The President sees things quite clearly and with mature reflection writes down the list of those insurgents who deserve decapitation.

German Arciniegas

In the courtyard David points out a famous murderer to me. They call him *Lombroso* because he's got the face of an angel. The man doesn't inspire fear but horror. At the head of a band of outlaws he attacked a small village and murdered twelve people, both defensive and indefensive: three nuns, six policemen, two children, and one mentally retarded person.

Looking at Lombroso, Mister Alba says to me:

"The murderers are starting to arrive. The murderers can't even leave the jail in peace anymore."

"They'll be releasing him for lack of proof pretty soon," David tells Mister Alba.

"They shouldn't bother arresting that kind of murderer or bringing him to trial."

"What should they do with them?"

"Wipe them off the face of the earth wherever they find them. They're at war with the law. The law can't face up to them through justice, it can only face up to them by waging war on them."

"If they do that the whole country will rise up in their defense in the name of justice."

"You can defend the living in the name of justice but not the dead."

"I feel pity for that man, the way I do for all prisoners."

"That's why the jail is the way it is," Mister Alba concludes. "For my part, I know how to control my compassion. I share in all the world's grief. I'm stirred by the pain of the condemned man, but I'm also stirred by the pain of the victim."

After meditating for a moment, Mister Alba says to me:

"With this prisoner and this attack, the gallery of dead people in your book has had a lot of enrichment."

"Those dead people out there in freedom affect me in a different way," I say. "It's as if I'd killed them myself."

"In that respect I'm at peace," Mister Alba states. "I only feel responsible for my own crimes."

"Those dead people belong to me," I insist. "From today on those dead will be part of my family of dead. From today on those dead are my kin in this life."

David and Mister Alba then go on arguing about the guerrillas. According to Mister Alba the guerrilla wars that started up in the country in 1948 have passed through several distinct phases. The first was political in character; it sowed a romantic side and had something to do with man's fight for freedom. The second belongs unmistakably to ordinary crime and is connected to the imbalance in the country's progress where, while justice remains underdeveloped, crime attains its highest technical perfection. The third corresponds to the advantage taken of this situation of moral deterioration by Communist intervention directed from Cuba. According to this theory of Mister Alba's, the chain has strong links. From the political crime of subversion of the established order it passed

196

on to the ordinary crime of bandit attacks and from this to the international crime of foreign aggression.

How much truth there is in all of this I don't know. The only thing I know is that the three periods are identified by similar atrocities, and matching rage along with the repugnant Lombroso is the message that the guerrillas are sending us in prison. Just as on the outside they've almost put an end to freedom, our beloved jail, too, is beginning to be threatened by the senseless pressure of that dark current of violence. As I point out the above to Mister Alba and David, I finish by telling them:

"In any case, there's no need to complain. These are signs of the times. There aren't too many countries these days that have escaped this demented terror."

"The fact that other countries are suffering from similar evils doesn't justify our continuing to tolerate them," David says.

"Also, the evil of the violence is worse here than anywhere else," Mister Alba observes. "Every newspaper in the world is talking about us. The violence has made us fashionable. Along these lines I don't think we should be worrying that the truth of it is being spread through the world. Countries are known for what they produce and violence is our best national export."

I try to refute this opinion, but Mister Alba cuts off any possibility of polemic by stating:

"What we're talking about has nothing to do with the jail. Violence is a typical phenomenon of freedom. The jail knows how to live in peace."

"What about the riot?" David asks.

"The prison riot wasn't an act of violence but a strike against the rules," Mister Alba maintains.

Later on, in the cell, we continue talking about the national insecurity caused by guerrilla bands and the general instability brought on by the economic crisis. In

197

jail the subject of the guerrillas is the topic of the day. David states that outside the jail people think the situation is so bad there's danger of a military government taking over.

"Ever since I was five years old I've been hearing people complain about the bad economic situation and the danger of a military coup," Mister Alba says.

"Don't you believe in that danger now?" I ask.

"In the first place, it's not a danger. It might be a solution. In the second place, military coups are always brought about for some reason. A good government is a strong government against which military coups are impossible."

"I didn't know you were a militarist, Mister Alba."

"I'm not a militarist. I follow realities, which is something else. The military coups of the past, when some bold colonel rose up into power and went about stealing from up there, are things of the past. Coups today are produced by unavoidable national exigencies."

"Listen to the founding father of freedom," David says.

"For military men to dislodge an honest and competent man from the government is and always will be a crime. But to dislodge someone immoral or inept seems to me to be an exercise in democracy just as respectable as that of someone who reaches power by votes in order to sleep or prosper there. The vote isn't always a guarantee of success either for the one doing the electing or the one elected."

"According to Mister Alba popular suffrage could be replaced with suffrage by dagger," David insists.

"I'm not a militarist," Mister Alba states again. "All of us prisoners are generally anti-militarist. But nor will I accept the idea of a democracy that thinks it has all rights when there have been errors at the polls. The military man who goes after power is no less despicable than the politician who subverts the voting process or the office-holder

198

who uses the vote to perpetuate himself in office. Between two bandits I prefer the one who's been trained for order. If patriotism has taken refuge in the barracks today, the blame doesn't lie with the jail but with the free men who can't exercise it or honor it. If democracy has taken refuge in the military today, the blame lies only with those on the outside who've taken it upon themselves to cheapen and discredit it."

This subject makes David furious. So as not to take part in the discussion he goes to the window and takes it upon himself to observe the courtyard. Mister Alba comments:

"I've demonstrated what I wanted to demonstrate. I don't agree with my own words, but I've used this way to demonstrate that David is a democrat even in this business of eluding the defense of democracy."

A rapid dialogue immediately develops between Mister Alba and the Honorable Fatso Tudela and I can't capture it completely.

"Between arms and letters, which do you favor?" Fatso asks.

"The battle isn't between arms and letters. Letters have surrendered. They went under when military men discovered that they could learn to read. The fight is now between arms and the masses. It's between military men and illiterates now."

"Between these two extremes, which side are you on?"

"Between these two pits there's no way out for me but to be neutral."

"Do you think that we'll be able to get rid of military men someday?" Fatso asks.

"There's no riddance to military men ever," Mister Alba replies.

"I read in a magazine there's no more need for military men in the modern world."

"The military will always be needed."

"What for?"

"For waging war."

"War against whom?"

"War against whom else? War against the Communists. War to protect us from the Communists and terrorists."

"And who's going to protect us from the military?"

"Other military men."

Fatso has doubts for a moment but returns to the attack.

"I'd like for armies to discharge their troops, for the barracks to be turned into schools, for obligatory military service to be eliminated, for the war budget to be spent on the development of wheat growing."

Mister Alba says:

"Answer me this: if we do away with the military, what are we going to do with the weapons?"

Fatso hesitates a little. In the end he can't answer. While he's still pondering, the cell door opens. Once more three armed guards are forming a ring of rifles and bayonets around a group of people. This time it's a matter of a very ugly old woman and a very pretty young one, along with two men with the faces of retired jailers.

"If I'm not mistaken," Mister Alba says, "we're being honored by another visit from the Society of Friends of Prisons."

"Not exactly," a guard states.

One of the strangers, a small bald man picks up the conversation:

"This time it's a matter of a personal initiative on the part of the warden meant to let the prisoners have some fun."

"Fun?" the Honorable Fatso Tudela asks.

"Yes. The warden, rightly upset by our jail's state of neglect has taken the happy initiative of bringing in a bit of fun for the inmates. This campaign has the support of the Ministers of Justice and National Education. We're going to show some movies about the Passion of the Lord. We'll have lectures on the lives of the great German composers. The problem of the jails is first and foremost a problem of education. But what I've just mentioned are part of the plans for the future."

"Might we know what plans the warden has for the present?"

"For the present," the bald man goes on, "the warden has decided to organize a beauty contest."

"That's a good idea, organizing a beauty contest among the prisoners," David says.

"It's not among the prisoners," the bald man corrects him.

"Is it among some female prisoners then?"

The bald man pays no attention to David and keeps on talking:

"At the moment you have the candidate here. Her name is Mercedes. When she's elected her official name will be Mercedes the First, Queen of the Jail."

Nobody in the cell gives a cheer for the queen but we all look at the candidate who, as a candidate, offers very a promising physical perspective. The Honorable Fatso Tudela asks:

"Does the young lady belong to the women's jail?"

"Why do you ask?" the bald man says.

"Because of what my distinguished colleague here, David Fresno, said. In order to be a candidate for the jail I thought that's how it would have to be," Fatso explains, somewhat perturbed.

"Well, no," the bald man assures him with great delicacy. "The young lady is a stenographer. She's the warden's secretary. Besides that, the warden is her father."

Mister Alba hastens to Fatso's aid, looking at the older lady and asking in turn:

"And who is this worthy lady?"

"She's the candidate's mother," the bald man states.

"I thought she was a candidate, too," Mister Alba says.

"A candidate?" the one referred to says softly, obviously flattered by Mister Alba's compliment.

"Yes," Mister Alba says. "You've got the face candidate. We could proclaim you Queen of Violence."

Visibly displeased now, she addresses her daughter:

"That's what we get for showing a little charity to prisoners."

The bald man doesn't understand what's going on or pretends that he doesn't. On the other hand, the man with him has to make a great effort not to burst out laughing. He takes out a handkerchief and starts chewing on it while the authentic candidate, the pretty stenographer, shows off her best movie expressions with teeth and eyes for the prisoners.

Nevertheless, so that people won't think badly of him, the bald man gives proof of his loyalty to the warden.

"You people could at least show a little respect for the warden. You could demonstrate that in spite of everything you have good feelings."

"As for respecting the warden, we respect him," Mister Alba says. "Good feelings, those we have. But we can't demonstrate good feelings. Good feelings have no place in the novel."

"I didn't know that jail was like this," the older lady says.

Mister Alba sighs.

"Jail is jail," he says. "Everything else is Civil Law."

"Well," the bald man says softly, "What do you say?"

"What do you want us to say?" David asks.

"Do you like the candidate or don't you?"

"If it's a question of that, we like her," Mister Alba says, interpreting the general feelings very accurately.

"All right," the bald man concludes. "The voting is over in this cell. The vote couldn't have been better. Four votes for Mercedes the First. The warden is going to feel very proud, not just for his daughter's success but also for the results of the first truly free elections to have taken place in the jail. There's no doubt. She'll be elected unanimously. Gentlemen, the party's over."

The party moves off, leaving us alone and carrying all its merriment with it. Still, at this moment I feel the way captives in the Middle Ages felt when a general amnesty was decreed for the birthday of the king's daughter.

We all wait for one of those philosophical conclusions that Mister Alba always derives from situations like the one we just experienced. Mister Alba meditates, but doesn't speak. David opens the way for him to say something.

"What's your opinion of beauty contests, Mister Alba?"

"Beauty contests are the atomic version of the white slave traffic," Mister Alba says.

David laughs and the Honorable Fatso Tudela comments:

"In any case, Her Majesty Mercedes the First isn't so bad."

"She isn't so bad," David says, "but she'd be a lot better without her mother. With her mom by her side I can't find anywhere the fun they want to bring the prisoners ."

"Candidates for beauty queen should be prohibited from having moms," Mister Alba concludes.

David, Mister Alba, and the Honorable Fatso Tudela keep on talking about beauty contests until the bell rings. According to Mister Alba, since democracy is the political system that lets us sigh for monarchy, beauty queens are the way in which democrats express their nostalgia for slavery. The theme brings them to discuss the juries that judge this type of contest. And juries bring them to the topic of public trials in which defendants are judged.

I don't know which of them proposes that we hold a trial in the cell to judge the conduct of the prisoners during the riot. I'm very tired. I don't pay any attention to the stupid idea. But the three of them decide to begin a trial to shed light on the death of Leloya.

This is the first time I hear my trial mentioned.

SUNDAY, NOVEMBER 22

A murderer is someone who remains dead in the one he has killed.
  Ramón Gómez de la Serna

Speaking to Mister Alba, the Honorable Fatso Tudela says:
  "First off, let's organize the court. Who is the accused?"
  "Who else could it be? Antón Castán. Why do you ask?"
  "I ask because any one of us could have assumed that responsibility successfully."
  "It's the matter of Leloya's death," Mister Alba points out. "The accused is Antón."
  "Take a look at David's face. He's got the unmistakable face of an accused man."
  "Don't insist, Fatso. The accused is Antón. We can't take that honor away from him."
  Fatso Tudela won't admit defeat.
  "As far as I know, no one saw how things happened. In that case, the first question we've got to ask is, 'Who killed Leloya?'"
  "That question would be fine in a detective story," David says. "But it's not a question for a play like this."
  "We're not trying to find out here who killed him, but why he killed him," Mister Alba says, straightening things out. "As David has just pointed out, this isn't a detective

205

story. The whole business is a lot more important. It's not a matter of a police case, but an examination of intent. It's not a matter of solving a mystery but of revealing the reasons behind it."

Nodding his head affirmatively, the Honorable Fatso Tudela finally accepts Mister Alba's arguments. But he immediately asks:

"What about the judge? Who's going to be the judge?"

"The judge is obvious, too," David says. "There's only one person in the cell who can be judge."

"Who?" Mister Alba asks, taken with the vague hope that David is referring to him.

"Who else?" David continues. "The only honorable prisoner here. I mean His Honor Fatso Tudela. Besides, he's got an additional advantage. He was a detective, so that when he makes a decision it will be very easy for him to be wrong."

Mister Alba makes his decision:

"David's right. The judge has got to be the Honorable Fatso Tudela."

The one referred to asks:

"What about spectators... Who's going to represent public opinion?"

"Let's go step by step," Mister Alba says. "First let's discuss the defense attorney."

Fatso Tudela won't let him go on:

"If we're going to go step by step, let's start with the prosecutor."

"That's right," Mister Alba agrees. "Who should be the prosecutor?"

David says:

"I don't see how you can have any doubts about that. There's only one man for that job here and that's you yourself, Mister Alba. Can you people conceive of Mister Alba defending a just cause or handing down justice in the name of the Republic under the authority of the law? Nobody here can challenge you for the privilege of accusing someone, Mister Alba."

"That means that you expect to handle the defense, David," Fatso Tudela deduces.

"Precisely."

"If that's how it is, I wouldn't bet on the accused getting off," Mister Alba concludes, anticipating the sweet taste of a hypothetical victory.

"We'll see about that," David says.

Mister Alba and David look at each other with a fierce and sharp rancor, very much like the one fighting cocks display before flying in to rake out each other's eyes. Fatso Tudela is beginning to enjoy the prospect of the duel between the two of them. He rubs his hands in satisfaction. But his enthusiasm suddenly comes to a halt. Fatso, who already feels himself judge, still has doubts about the composition of the court.

"Who's going to play the role of the jury? Who'll be the spectators? We've used up all the available people in the cell."

David asks:

"Why spectators?"

"What else for?" Fatso Tudela asks. "To applaud, which is what public opinion is for. Besides, public opinion boosts the authority of the judge. Just so they won't forget him, the judge has to threaten the public that attends trials every so often."

"I can understand a jury," David says, "but there's no need for public opinion in jail. We'll proceed like it was a matter of a secret trial."

"I've got an idea," Mister Alba offers. "The guard can play the part of a moral jury."

"But the guard hasn't got any morality," David says.

"Exactly," Mister Alba assures him. "That's why the guard is the best one for that role. He's perfect for putting together an improvised judgment without knowing what it's all about. That is, he's perfect for seeing that justice is done."

The Honorable Fatso Tudela goes to the door. Through the grating, where the small door is open, the guard has been listening to everything being said in the cell. Fatso Tudela speaks to the guard through the grating:

"We want to ask a favor of you. We've just organized a trial to be held in the cell. To see that justice is done. All that's missing is a jury."

The guard shows signs of indignation. He replies:

"I wouldn't want to fall into the hands of any court made up of murderers and counterfeiters and swindlers."

"Do you think the trials held on the outside are any better?" David asks him.

"On the outside at least they know what's right and what's wrong," the guard maintains.

Mister Alba crushes him with his look as he says:

"Only God knows what's right and what's wrong. And God doesn't take part in any trials."

The guard speaks with even greater annoyance:

"In any case, I'm not having any part in what you people are planning. Watching criminals mocking justice disgusts me."

"Don't exaggerate," Mister Alba says.

"I'm completely opposed to criminals spitting on the law and insulting the dignity of the nation," the guard says, red with rage.

David becomes wheedling and conciliatory. He talks to the guard in his softest tone of voice:

"I don't know where you get so many scruples from, guard. You should understand that what we're doing here is only a reflection of what's done outside. Our beloved jail is the mirror of freedom: the shame of innocent people in jail is in direction proportion to the infamy that there are criminals free outside. Go out into the street and take a look in any direction and see if men who are free are giving the nation's dignity any thing better than what we've given it: robbery, violence, atrocities, infamy, terror. Ask Antón Castán what he thinks about outside justice and then tell me if in our beloved jail it's forbidden to imitate justice. Let us have our little trial, guard."

"Do whatever you want," the guard says.

He moves away from the door, but suddenly he repents and returns. Now he's bursting with a just and patriotic rage. He draws his revolver and points it into the cell through the grating. Unable to restrain himself, he threatens:

"If anyone says a single word I'll put a bullet in his head."

In a situation like that, under that kind of police protection, the prisoners involved in the trial can do nothing but remain silent. None of them says anything. All of them, accused, prosecutor, defense attorney, and even the judge himself have no choice but to remain silent.

In that reign of silence I think about the court surrounding me. I don't know why, but I'm afraid of them. In a certain way this court isn't any farce for me. There's something legitimate about it, something quite real. Instead of the friendly feeling that my companions surrounded me with before, something is separating me from them now, and that something is the barrier that separates the prisoner from the court.

When finally, quite some time after, tired of pointing his revolver at us, the guard goes away, David comments:

"Cops don't understand theater. Today's a day that's been lost for justice."

Mister Alba also draws a conclusion from the guard's compulsion and says:

"It's better that there hasn't been any justice today. Since we don't have any freedom we don't need any justice either."

MONDAY, NOVEMBER 23

There's nothing that makes us more unbearable than calling a murderer
a murderer and an innocent person innocent.

    François Mauriac

With the four of us sitting on the beds my knees almost
touch David's. The trial is about to begin.

"Who has the Holy Bible?" the Honorable Fatso Tudela
asks.

"What do you want the Holy Bible for?" Mister Alba
asks in turn.

"To administer the oaths."

"Mister Alba has a Bible but it's not holy because it's
not Catholic," David says.

"That doesn't matter," the judge decrees. "Since the
latest reform of the Church the Protestants have become
our brothers. As it's not for reading but for swearing, any
Bible is good just so long as it's a Bible."

Mister Alba goes to the corner where he has his books
stacked, gets the Bible, and gives it to Fatso. The latter
glances at it and, realizing that it's an English version,
hesitates a little. He asks:

"Are you a Protestant, Mister Alba?"

"I'm not a Protestant, but I'm interested in Protestant
things, just the way I'm interested in the beliefs of all men.

I'm not homosexual, but I've read Croydon. I'm not a cowboy either, but I know all of Zane Grey's books."

"How can I know if it's really the Bible?" Fatso asks.

"You can be sure. The courts in London take the oath on this same one."

Fatso accepts. With the Bible in his hand he stands up, raises his arm, and says these words:

"Mister Alba, do you swear to fulfill honestly and faithfully your duties as prosecutor? That is, do you swear to prosecute, prosecute, and prosecute until there's nothing left to prosecute?"

"I swear," Mister Alba says, letting himself be carried away by the fiction, making a cross with his fingers and raising them to his mouth after touching the Bible.

After this scene I again get the feeling that I'm in a genuine trial.

Fatso sits down again and Mister Alba starts talking. I can feel the weight of the accusation that's only beginning on my shoulders. Mister Alba seems to have forgotten about David and me and he's addressing the Honorable Fatso Tudela as if he were speaking to him alone.

"Your Honor must permit me to leave out certain details that are usual in cases like this. I've been prosecuted many times and therefore I know how a prosecution proceeds. Today, as I see it, the facts are quite simple. On the last day of the riot, in the offices of the jail, one man killed another. The dead man is in the cemetery. The murderer is in this cell. We are going to pass judgment on him and in order to do so we are going to find out something that has not been clear up till now. Why did Antón Castán kill? Why did he kill? Our decision will be easy, our justice will be just if we succeed in answering this question."

Seated, I'm getting a bit nervous. For the first time I hear myself being called a murderer. That moves Mister

Alba to take notice of me. I can see that he's looking at me with reproachful eyes, which I'd never seen in him before. Mister Alba takes off his hat and puts it on again with that gesture which is characteristic in him when he's speaking in public.

"Would the prosecutor stop talking with his hat on?" the judge requests.

"Your Honor will have to forgive me," the prosecutor says. "If I take off my hat it will be the same as taking off my head. I come from a long line of conquerors, that is, I come from a long line of men who think and work with their hats on. If I take off my hat I won't be able to speak."

Mister Alba clears his throat and continues:

"In the attempt to clarify why this man killed, I shall paint a picture of the truth for Your Honor. Let us say that Antón Castán killed because he was innocent. Tired of being innocent and paying in jail for a crime he didn't commit, Antón decided to kill Leloya. He wanted to remove the smell of innocence from his body and bloodstains can only take that away. Is this the truth? Yes, it is. It is for me and therefore I ask that Antón Castán be sentenced to life imprisonment. Antón should not have killed. Freedom was created so that a man can lose his innocence. But in prison a man has no right to cease being innocent."

He puts in his monocle, in his good eye this time. It's obvious that he's all excited. He immediately again starts speaking:

"Did Antón Castán kill because jail corrupted him? Here is the truth again. What is Your Honor going to do with so much truth? There's nothing more oppressive than the truth. How nice a little lying would feel right now! Well, the truth is, Your Honor, that jail corrupted Antón Castán. Three years of living together with murderers and thieves has had its effect. Antón wasn't only innocent; he was also

213

pure. Jail has already laid its rotten eggs in this immaculate nest. I ask that Antón Castán be found not guilty. And I ask that we punish the only guilty party. I ask that we put the jail in jail."

Since I have David directly opposite me, we both keep looking at each other. I don't see him as David now but as my defense attorney. Once more our eyes speak through our silence. Our eyes share the secret of the deepest human feelings. Mister Alba is going ahead now with another chapter of his dissertation.

"It can also be maintained that Antón killed because he hated Leloya. It's not worth our time ascertaining why he hated him. Hate clogged up his body, the fury of his hate paralyzed his blood. He couldn't sleep because he didn't want to waste the time he could be hating him. He killed, therefore, in order to stop hating him and to find some rest from his rancor. I would swear that he killed in order to get some sleep. I don't know what the appropriate punishment might be for this case. I imagine that the Penal Code doesn't indicate what's to be done with a man who kills in order to get some sleep."

Mister Alba takes a moment to recover from a weakness in his voice, which has caused him to cough a few times. The crisis over, he continues speaking, more forcefully:

"But there's no doubt that Antón didn't kill Leloya for being Leloya but for being the warden of the jail. His hand performed an act that had been shaped by the lamentations of the centuries, his hand held the demands of all the wretched of the earth. In Leloya, he killed the dictatorship of jails, the age-old regime of prisons, the oppression of chains, the technical remains of slavery. A half century ago Master Vargas Vila defined Antón Castán's crime: 'I only feel guilty of one crime, the crime that Caesar is still alive.' So, therefore, Antón, being innocent, began to feel guilty

214

of the crime that Caesar was still alive, and for Caesar not to be alive, he killed him in Leloya. Antón Castán is the assassin of all tyranny. His crime is a political crime. I ask that we sentence him to freedom."

Mister Alba looks weary. He pauses and takes a deep breath. It's clear that he's coming to the end.

"Your Honor has four truths to choose from. But bull-fighters say that the fifth truth is the real truth. Here is the fifth truth for Your Honor. Do not smile, Your Honor, if I assure you that Anton killed for a purely literary motive. I might also say that he killed in a gesture of nicety. David Fresno thinks that what he's writing is a play. There can be no doubt here that Antón killed Leloya in order to end the second act of his play successfully. Just as the writers of novels who kill in theory in order to set forth a thesis or to give their books an aura of mystery. Antón really killed in order to give his imprisoned innocence the stamp of a little pathos. With this death his book will be able to have more copies sold. I ask a literary purging for him. I ask for him the punishment that a Caribbean tyrant once imposed on writers: he would let them publish a book, but then he would make them eat it."

Looking toward the cell door, Mister Alba gets ready to continue, but his voice disappears into his throat. The accusation has ended. Through the grillwork the small outer door is open now. Two feverish eyes scrutinize the cell. Today the guard doesn't need to point his revolver at us to make us be silent.

TUESDAY, NOVEMBER 24

When a man shoots at another, he's shooting at himself:
there are no such things as murderers in the world.

   Curzio Malaparte

"The defense has the floor," says the Honorable Fatso
Tudela after swearing David in.

David looks nervous, as if he were facing an audience.
He starts speaking in a low voice:

"I shouldn't bother with the accusation because, as a
simple matter of fact, there's been no accusation here. But
because of the respect I have for the jail and from the
necessity I have to make apologies to it, I am obliged to
examine Mister Alba's fallacious statements one by one. I
can't do otherwise. I'm going to jump into the swamp. I'm
going to destroy the many-colored riddles that Mister Alba
has tried to dazzle us with. I shall do it with a slap of the
hand, the way a child knocks the scattered pieces of a
domino game onto the floor."

David speaks without a pause. I don't look at him now.
I feel calm, almost free. His voice is sheltering me from
the fear of the unknown.

"Mister Alba has shown us the five faces of truth. But
when truth shows us five faces it's because it no longer

feels sure that it is the truth. To say that Antón killed in order to cleanse his body of the stench of innocence is to befoul innocence with incredible perversity. To say that he killed because the jail corrupted him is to slander the jail. To say that he killed in order to get some sleep is a Russian fable: Mister Alba read that in a book by Chekhov I loaned him a little while ago. To say that he killed out of inspiration by Master Vargas Vila is to support the idea that the crime was committed by the only disciple that Vargas Vila has here, Mister Alba, that is. To say that he killed in order to give a touch of tragedy to the second act of the play is a case of not knowing anything about this cell. Ever since Mister Alba came into it this cell has no longer had any need of more tragedy."

At this point David's voice, although still low, becomes more forceful:

"Using the same criterion of coining truths with the metal of lies, I could also present other aspects of that matter that Mister Alba has omitted. I could prove, for example, that Leloya isn't dead, even though they've buried him, because his deeds, his crimes that is, are alive. I could say that Antón didn't kill him but that it was Mister Alba himself or whoever it was set up a meeting with him at the spot where he met his death. I could show that Antón's arm of flesh and blood didn't kill Leloya, but that Oscar's wooden leg did. I could say that the crime has temporal and transmigratory antecedents, and I could state that when he killed, Antón was fulfilling a predestination that came to him out of the deepest commitments of an ancient incarnation. The honorable judge told the Catholic ladies that Leloya committed suicide. Without throwing out such a hypothesis it wouldn't be hard to bring out the fact that it wasn't Leloya who died in Leloya but Antón Castán himself. I could also have recourse to a purely dramatic interpretation, proving that Antón killed because he loves the publicity of a trial, that is, he killed in order to be tried. Following another track I could be qualified to show that he killed out of humanitarian compassion: he killed in order to save Leloya from the horror of being a victim of an atomic war. Finally, it wouldn't be hard for me to place in evidence the fact that by killing Leloya, Antón saved himself from being killed by Leloya; it's possible that Leloya was made warden of the jail in order to wipe out the traces of an old slander against Antón with a new crime."

He's perspiring so much that the wet cloth of his shirt is sticking to his ribs, making the outline of his bones stand out like a hazy X-ray.

"In a real trial the exposition and development of any of these versions would be a triumph of penal science, but here it's a question of bringing ghosts to life. Here it's not a matter of turning the laws into a juggler's show. In this phantom court I can only believe in man."

David is speaking vigorously now. Under the pounding of his voice Mister Alba's burned-out eye looks like a hollow filled with ashes.

"I'm not defending the man. I'm trying to understand the man's actions. And since I'm trying to understand them, in this case I can tell you, finally, the truth. It's the only truth. Antón Castán killed in order to perform an act of vengeance."

In the shadows I can feel the dead beginning to stir. The dead... Why haven't I spoken of the dead until now?

The dead are afraid of the prisoners but they come to the cell quite often. Sometimes, when I feel myself alone, I whistle up the dead. I whistle them up the way my father used to whistle to his dogs, calling them when he had to take them out to hunt down prisoners who'd escaped from

218

his jail. And, like my father's dogs, the dead hear my call, arrive obediently, and lie down by my feet. Justice has left its fingerprints in the jail and those prints are the dead who fill the life of the jail.

One night I whistled in the cell and Mister Alba asked me:

"What are you whistling for, Antón?"

"I'm calling the dead," I said.

"If they're dead they won't be coming."

"They're dead but they come to live with us when I call them."

"I don't get it."

"Murderers never die. They go on living in their crimes. For a murderer, jail is immortality. When a man kills another they both go to jail. The dead also have a subconscious and that subconscious of the dead is what's alive among us."

Mister Alba got up from his bed. Braulio, too, moved about in his. The two of them must have thought I was crazy. But I wasn't upset because I knew that David understood me and that the dead also understood me.

Now the dead are here without my having called them. Or maybe I called them without realizing it and they came thinking that I needed them. In any case, I can feel the cold of their breath very close to me. Today they lick my hands too, as if the dead were looking for some bread in my hands. You mustn't believe that they've come to accuse me. They've come to defend me. I'm a prisoner, which means that I belong to them. On my fingers, as the dead are licking my hands, I can feel quite clearly the damp and manly brush of my father's dead lips.

Far away, even though he's near me, David continues talking. Maybe the dead have had an influence on him because his voice has an accent from beyond the grave.

"I'm not going to tell you that with Leloya's death Antón Castán got his revenge on the system of justice. Nor am I going to tell you that Antón killed in order to play a trick on freedom by getting back for himself the freedom to kill. I will even have less to tell you about fate's taking charge by placing Oscar's leg within reach of the destroying arm. No. My ideas about Leloya's death are so simple that because of their very simplicity they border on the half-witted. I don't want to give Your Honor a headache by telling you that after he strangled his lover, Leloya managed to put Antón Castán in jail, accusing him of his crime. Lawyer Ramírez revealed that secret to Antón. Leloya was the political boss and in our town the boss owns freedom. When Leloya was named warden of the jail, Antón must have begun to feel that death was getting close to him. When the riot broke out and he had him right there death was already trickling through his fingers like sweat. I've said it all: it's as simple as the truth. It's as simple as a lie. It's as simple as justice. Justice is pure and it's simple, but men complicated and befouled it when they turned it into jail. And since this case is so simple I'm not asking for the acquittal or the conviction of the accused. I ask that we look for the way to understand it, because this will be the only way to absolve justice. In that way we'll be able to apply to this individual contest the criminal logic of historic battles, after which jails will be shutdown and statues uncovered. All of this leads me to conclude that Antón Castán has not committed any crime. He has simply won. Leloya had rebelled against the rights of man by persecuting Antón Castán. When he killed him in the jail, Antón won the war. The war's over: make way for the victor. The time has come for handing out medals."

He remains standing after these last words. Next to me the dead are agitated, excited, impatient, wild, like the dogs when my father was getting ready to go out and hunt down escaped prisoners. The dead are brushing against my legs with their hairy rumps, as though they wanted to invite me to leave the cell, as though they wanted me to follow them along the pathways of death.

The judge asks:

"Does the prosecution have anything to declare?"

Mister Alba replies:

"The only thing I have to say is that it's a shame David wasn't able to finish his studies at the university because he went to jail. The defense attorney speaks as well, or even better said, speaks as badly as a lawyer."

The voice of the Honorable Fatso Tudela rings out very clearly:

"The accused has the floor."

I have nothing to say in this trial. Still, the dead ask me to speak. Maybe they're barking with their dusty jaws to ask me, but in some way they're demanding it. It would please the dead if I were to speak. They calm down with the sound of my voice. At times while I'm speaking they go to sleep at my feet. They begin to dream that they're alive then.

In any case, I wouldn't have spoken if I hadn't noticed suddenly that among the dead curled about my feet is Leloya. At first I want to step on him, give him a scare. I hadn't counted on that dead person. But when I feel again the warm and yet dead tongue of my father on my hands, I have an inspiration. I decide to upset Leloya:

"I'm innocent," I say in a loud voice.

All of them, the living and the dead, look at me with surprise. Only Leloya looks at me with fear. I say:

"Your Honor, please give the victim the floor now."

"Who?"

"The victim, the dead man."

I've never seen the Honorable Fatso Tudela so confused.

"What did you say?"

"I said that maybe the dead man has something to say."

"Where's the dead man?"

"He's here. The dead are always where they judge the dead. Give him the floor and he'll talk. Leloya's testimony is fundamental in this case."

His Honor makes no decision in spite of the fact that Mister Alba also asks that we hear Leloya.

Meanwhile Leloya stays there crouching like a dog ready to spring at the throat of his enemy. But Leloya doesn't spring at my throat. When he hears that Mister Alba has asked that he speak, he realizes that not much is needed for us to start him talking. Suddenly he leaps up, but not to attack me, to run away. I understand quite well. The dead don't like to talk about their crimes.

The dead don't like to be called murderers when they're the ones who drive others to kill.

Given a boost by Leloya's flight, I repeat very clearly: "I'm innocent."

The pack of dead run after Leloya, nipping at his heels. It's pitiful. I can't hold them back. I'm exhausted. I haven't got the strength to whistle up the dead anymore.

WEDNESDAY, NOVEMBER 25

This accused is his own worst defender.
  Bruno Weil

The Honorable Fatso Tudela is getting ready to hand down his decision. All through the night before he was tossing in bed, bothered by the innumerable surprises that had come out in the course of the trial.

Today Fatso Tudela has more of a judge's face than on previous days. The closeness to the decision makes him impatient. There's no doubt that concern for the role he's been called upon to play in the trial is beginning to stamp him with character.

Quite early the judge starts writing his decision. There's one thing you can't reproach Fatso for as a judge and that's delaying the administration of the law.

I would have liked to hold back the judge's hand at this moment, to tell him that before he finishes writing the decision he remember that it was he himself, the judge, who stimulated the idea of killing in me. But the Honorable Fatso Tudela dedicates himself to literature and to justice with all his bodily energy. It's impossible at this moment for him to stop writing in order to recall the fateful question that he himself asked me that afternoon:

223

"Wouldn't you like to kill him?" And it mustn't be thought that I'm accusing the judge. I'm simply saying he started vibrating in the air the string of an idea whose firm end, the act of killing, had already been ripening inside me.

At one point the judge stops writing.

"How do you spell freedom?" he asks.

"Write it any way you want," Mister Alba says. "But write it in capital letters. Freedom is an important word."

Fatso continues writing. A half hour later he announces that he's ready to make his decision known. He immediately starts to read the finding:

"Familiar with the accusation and having heard the defense, I turn my full attention to the administration of justice. Neither side is of any help to justice in this case. The defense, because it includes too much; the prosecution because it hasn't pushed hard enough. It's too bad that the dead man didn't want to speak. As for the accused, he still has the nerve to maintain that he's innocent. I might have been prepared to accept that idea, but there's no doubt in my mind that it's become obvious that even if he is innocent, Leloya died in his arms, as we might say. In this trial the only thing that's clear is doubt. Everything is confused, so we have to accept the confusion. Not being able to punish him for the crime that he obviously committed, but not being able for that same reason to give his freedom back, I sentence Antón Castán to remain in jail and continue purging himself of the crime he didn't commit."

This isn't a judge's decision but one from a detective. But it's the decision that Mister Alba and David expected. Any other, based on the strict interpretation of justice, would have upset them.

For my part, I must say, too, that if during the moments of accusation and defense the judgment seemed legitimate to me, it doesn't seem that way so much now. At the time of sentencing the color we see things with changes. The judge's sentence, in fact, has had the virtue of opening my eyes. Once more I can see that the trial was a machination on the part of the jail to upset and confuse me.

Nevertheless, at this moment I feel naked before the members of the court. I've got nothing to hide from them. There is nothing to cover my most hidden secrets from the six eyes looking at me now. I've had this feeling of finding myself naked before justice before, at least twice in my life.

As a child I once suffered a shame like this. Near my house on the road between home and school, which I took every day, was Don Zimarro's store. He sold everything in his place. But there was one thing that even though it was for sale I couldn't own. It was a little red wind-up truck that howled like a fire engine when it ran. That truck, which my father either didn't want me to have or was unable to buy for me, obsessed me. I spent nights thinking about it. I spent hours contemplating it in the window of Don Zimarro's shop. I would have given anything to get it.

One day I decided to steal it. Don Zimarro was half-blind so distracting or fooling him would be quite easy. According to my calculations the work involved in getting the toy was only a matter of going into the store and coming out with it in my hand. I got to the store. Don Zimarro came out to meet me.

"Have you come to steal the truck?" he asked.

"How do you know what I've come for?" I asked in turn, frightened but without losing my composure.

"I dreamt last night that you would come and steal this toy today. The red truck, to be exact. It's so strange. Tell me the truth. I need for you to tell me the truth."

He seemed more concerned in finding out if the dream of the night before matched the reality of the present day than maintaining ownership of the toy.

In any case, I stole it. Since Don Zimarro knew that I was a thief, there was no reason to hide it. I went off with the toy right under Don Zimarro's nose. The old man looked at me, not moving, not protesting, not saying anything, as if he were still dreaming. Evidently that real action of which he'd had a presentiment in his dream had left him mute and paralyzed. As for me, for a person who had no daring whatever about him, it was all a revelation.

It was a heroic deed, but between the moment I went into the shop and the moment I came out with the toy, I felt that my heart held no secrets from Don Zimarro. It was more or less the same thing I'm feeling right now before the court since the judge has handed down his strange sentence.

Another time I felt naked in public was the day they arrested me. I was working at the oil refinery back there in Barranca. On weekends I would leave the refinery and go to my hometown. I don't know why I went there, since I no longer had any family or something to tie me to the place. Except for my father's grave, I had nothing in that town.

When I got off the bus three policemen came over to me and escorted me to the town jail. I couldn't get them to tell me why they were arresting me. It was only three years later, in prison that I succeeded in finding out. When I got off the bus, however, it looked to me as if they were arresting me simply because they had nothing else to do or that they were arresting me the way would arrest just anybody. That attitude of indifference on the part of the police was the only thing that made me remember at that moment that I was innocent.

Between the bus and the town jail where I was held, I first began to feel again what I'd felt under the implacable scrutiny of Don Zimarro's eyes. It didn't matter that this time I was completely innocent. The ones who watched

226

me go by on my way to jail between three cops had no way of knowing that I really was innocent. You don't carry innocence on your forehead like a star on a horse's brow. And yet people insulted me just by looking at me as if I had some mark on my forehead. Pablo Lepanto has said that a judge has to look with three pairs of eyes: the eyes on his face, the eyes of his mind, and the eyes of patience; because in that way, just as in the darkness of night, there's nothing that looks so much like a thief as a cop. When the truth isn't known there's nothing that looks so much like a guilty person than an innocent one.

As a child, when I watched them taking a man to jail, the scene was so ironic that it had a comic look about it. The man who was going to jail was a caricature of the man who was losing his freedom. The man who was going to jail made me laugh as a child the way children are made to laugh unconsciously by a man who slips and falls. On the way to jail, not as a spectator now but as someone under arrest, I couldn't get rid of the idea that some child somewhere might be laughing as he watched me pass. For me at that moment the only thing of any importance was the fact that children might be laughing at my innocence. And that childish laughter, anonymous but unavoidable, was right then and there revealing my intimate matters on the street as if the world were examining the X-ray of my soul.

Another idea that attacked me as they were taking me to jail was that even if I looked like it, I might not be completely innocent.

A man loves his innocence with the same absurd force with which he fears the crimes he's committed.

I discovered, too, that's what matters most isn't jail, but the road to jail. On the way to jail, I was searching desperately for the guilt that was laying that punishment on me. Still feeling myself innocent, I was attacked by the remorse of unknown crimes. It wasn't really that

I felt myself guilty, it was the fact that others were purifying themselves by thinking that all the blame fell on me.

Confused as it might seem, as I looked back at my three years in jail, harassed by men's hostile looks, I still felt responsible for countless crimes committed by other people. In that way I was fulfilling my family quota in the crimes of all men. People didn't see myself in me at that moment. They saw in me everyone who'd broken the law. There was no way I could hide the sins that weren't mine but belonged to everybody.

A guard comes to get me and takes me to the warden's office. As I go out it seems that my three companions are sure that the warden had sent for me in order to confirm the sentence. The warden receives me with Ramírez, my lawyer. When I get back to the cell they hound me with questions.

"What happened?"

"What did they say to you?"

"They told me I'm getting my freedom back tomorrow."

"What?" the three of them shout.

"That's it. They told me to get ready to leave tomorrow. The warden added that my good behavior helped a lot toward my release."

"Good behavior?" Mister Alba repeats, wrapping his tongue around the words letter by letter.

"Good behavior? Are you sure he said good behavior?" David asks.

"Yes," I said, putting an end to it. "I'm leaving tomorrow. I've just signed the papers for my release. I really should be leaving today. The papers carry today's date."

At first the Honorable Fatso Tudela has nothing to say. But I know what he's thinking. The judge can't understand why his decision isn't being carried out. In fact, a while later Fatso comments:

"I'm afraid there were deficiencies that are preventing the sentence from being carried out."

Mister Alba's protest over that decision of unconditional and immediate release brings on a strange reaction in him. Mister Alba picks up a pencil and writes something. Then he calls the guard and asks him to take that message to the warden.

"What's that all about?" the Honorable Fatso Tudela asks.

"I'm asking the warden to impose the death sentence on me."

"Why?" Fatso asks.

"All my life I've been accused of something. Now, for the first time it's fallen upon me to judge someone else and I've failed. I shouldn't live anymore. I deserve the death penalty."

"The death penalty doesn't exist in our system of justice," Fatso states.

"There are a lot of things that don't exist there and yet we talk about them as if they did."

"Is it a protest over what they're doing for Antón?"

"It's a protest over what they're doing to justice."

The Honorable Fatso Tudela lets a moment pass and comes out with this definitive thought:

"Sentences are no longer carried out, even in jail."

A little later, all worn out, Mister Alba has fallen asleep. I look at him with calm and compassion. He looks old to me, an old age that has burst forth out of his flesh and bones suddenly and unexpectedly. David takes advantage of the moment to tell me confidentially:

"I'm afraid they're going to have to transfer him to an asylum."

But Mister Alba isn't asleep, only pretending to be.

He opens his eyes and looks at David, without rancor, but without hope either. And he starts talking in a very muffled voice:

"In Málaga, where I was born, I met a philosopher once. He's the only philosopher I've ever seen face to face. His name was Donato Cruzado. Shortly before they took him off to the madhouse I heard him say something that's the best thing ever been said about life. Donato Cruzado said, 'If I wasn't crazy, I'd go crazy.'"

THURSDAY, NOVEMBER 26

A man only get his innocence back if he wins back his freedom.
  Henry Miller

While I'm packing my bag Mister Alba talks to me endlessly:

"Are you going to publish the book?"

"Of course. Prepare yourself for having people talk about you, Mister Alba."

"How are you going to get it out of the jail?"

"No problem. I've already asked my lawyer. If there are any objections he'll take care of everything. He's the warden's cousin."

"Who's going to publish the book?"

"I don't know. I'm going to give it to Ramírez, who told me that he'd take it to Pablo Lepanto, the writer. Maybe Lepanto will take an interest in it."

"If he takes it, Lepanto will be so interested that he'll publish it under his own name."

Not even in those moments, when he should have worried a little of what I'm going to think of him in the future, does Mister Alba look after his reputation. For Mister Alba there's nothing better than saying something nasty about his fellow man.

When Mister Alba leaves me for a moment the Honorable Fatso Tudela takes his turn in the farewell interrogation. I can't avoid it. The Honorable Fatso Tudela's mushy talk obliges me to turn sentimental.

"Will you come see us?"

"Of course I'll come to see you. I'll bring you all some books."

"Don't forget to pay a visit to my wife."

"I won't forget."

"I want you to get to know my children."

"Don't worry, I'll get to know them."

"They're good kids. They like to think of me in my job as a detective. Careful what you tell them. They don't know I'm in here. They think I'm out of the country on a secret mission. My children like to see me taking men to jail."

He's silent for a moment, ponders, and starts talking again:

"What plans do you have for your life, Antón?"

"I don't know what plans life will have for me."

"I mean... what kind of work are you going to do?"

I would have liked to tell him that jail had taught me how not to work. But I don't say anything. Still, the Honorable Fatso Tudela can't stop being concerned with the fate that awaits me on the outside.

"How are you going to make use of your freedom? What are you going to do?"

"I intend to sit down by the side of some lonely road and feel free and look at the sky and smile. That's all I intend doing."

"Be careful with lonely roads," Mister Alba says. "While you're smiling and looking at the sky the guerrillas might grab you."

To get away from the Honorable Fatso Tudela's topographical questions I turn to watering the rosebush. David follows me.

"Are you going to take the rose?"

"No. I'm leaving it here. Don't forget that it's for decorating your coffin."

David puts on a melancholy smile.

"I'll take good care of it."

He immediately goes on to express his worries about Mister Alba's health again.

"I think he's crazy."

"He's always been that way."

"No. Now he's really crazy. They'll have to take him to the asylum."

"Jail is the halfway point on the road between freedom and the asylum."

In spite of what I'm saying I can't conceive of Mister Alba in the crazy house. Not even for the benefit of the crazy house can I conceive of Mister Alba outside the jail.

"He's crazy," David repeats.

"He's not crazy, I'm sure of it."

"But he's not sane either."

"He isn't crazy and he isn't sane," I say in acceptance.

"If he isn't crazy and he isn't sane, what are they going to do with him?"

"Leave him in jail," I declare. "Jail's the only solution. Jail's the place for free men."

"What's a free man?"

"A man who isn't crazy but isn't sane either." I finish with the rose and tell David:

"Cultivate it. It'll look nice on top of your coffin. Keep on watering it. It'll bloom someday. Why shouldn't it bloom?"

Behind me, following the few steps I can take in the cell, David doesn't leave me. He looks like a child following a father who's getting ready to take a trip. He asks me:

"What are you going to tell Nancy?"

"I don't know Nancy."

233

"She knows you and she likes you."

"So what's that to me?"

"I can tell when Nancy likes a man."

"In any case, I won't be seeing her."

"She'll come for you."

"Let's change the subject, David"

"She'll come to get you in the Ford. She's probably already waiting for you on the corner."

"She doesn't know I'm getting out."

"Women know when men are getting out of jail."

"David, I don't know Nancy and it's no concern of mine. Stop talking about it."

But he's getting more and more excited over the possibility that freedom will bring me close to Nancy. Freedom for him at this moment is the country where Nancy is going to meet me, the country where only Nancy and I will be living.

"If you go out riding with her, don't the two of you get on the same horse. If you don't want to go crazy, don't the both of you ride the same horse."

"Don't pay any attention to him, Antón. The poor fellow's crazy," Mister Alba says in a protective tone.

"Who has any sanity in here?" I ask.

"Everybody has his sanity because everybody's lost his sanity," Mister Alba says.

All that's left for me to do is say goodbye to the dead. But I don't dare whistle them up. If I do maybe they'll want to go with me, leaping along the paths of freedom like my father's dogs when he went out into the countryside hunting down prisoners. I don't want any freedom for the dead. At least I don't want any freedom for me with the dead.

Mister Alba asks me:

"Are you coming to the dedication of the monument?"

"What monument?"

"Don't you know about it? The monument to the unidentified prisoner. It will consist of a mausoleum, crowned by Oscar's leg."

"That's right," David observes. "The warden's given his permission for the monument to be built. The warden's crazy, too."

The Honorable Fatso Tudela says with conviction:

"When I get out look me up in Medellín. It'll be easy to find me. Ask for me at the detective squad, the Medellín section."

For the last time David puts in:

"Nancy's already on the corner waiting for you."

I put the pages of the diary into the suitcase. I close it and get ready to leave.

Mister Alba says:

"It's a novel. We can write the words The End."

"It's a play," David insists. "You'll have to say, Curtain Falls."

The Honorable Fatso Tudela, who's not in on the literary secrets of the cell, is looking at us as if, indeed, we all were really crazy.

The guard who's come to get me opens the door. Getting freedom back has one advantage, the fact that if we never remember how we came into the jail, we can remember every step of how we leave.

As the door is closed from the outside, I open the peephole. I can take that liberty just as though I were a guard because I'm no longer an inmate.

I don't know how I could look at that den of iniquity without screaming. Maybe freedom is beginning to confuse me. Inside, David, Mister Alba, and the Honorable Fatso Tudela are pitiful figures. They look like animals in a zoo. Only at that moment do I discover that, in addition

235

to everything else, caged, defenseless prisoners are characters in a rather comical exhibition.

Suddenly something makes me shudder. When they realize that I'm leaving, next to Mister Alba, next to David, next to the Honorable Fatso Tudela, the dead begin to grow restless. To my great surprise I discover from the outside that I'm still inside, but not with the living anymore, with the dead. There I am with that poor dead inmate that Leloya is now. There I am with the dead who lick my hands, looking for the bread of the dead in them. The cell is full of corpses. The cell is the cemetery of the men who seal peace with justice.

My presence among the dead is no obsession. Outside I feel pitifully alone, as if I was free but my innocence was back in jail.

When I finally leave I know that there in the midst of those prisoners and those dead I'm leaving behind the corpse of my freedom.